"Well played!" Admiration danced in Cole's blue eyes. **"You helped convince Becca I'm off the market—I could kiss you."**

Kate inhaled sharply, but it didn't seem to put any air in her lungs. "It's, ah, probably best if you don't." She started to take a step backward.

"Oh, I don't know." His voice dropped lower. "Becca's got spies everywhere."

"Cole, I..." Her voice was husky, unfamiliar. Though he was no longer touching her, he stood so close her thoughts were short-circuiting. Could she allow herself to kiss him in the name of convincing Becca he was taken? A flimsy excuse, at best, but so tempting. She swallowed. "I have to go."

"Can I call you later? We didn't finish our conversation."

She lifted up on her toes, pressing a quick kiss against his cheek. It was a peck, nothing more, but effervescent giddiness fizzed through her. She'd surprised herself—and she could tell from his sudden, absolute stillness that she'd shocked him.

"Just in case any of Becca's spies are watching," she murmured.

Dear Reader,

Falling in love isn't always easy. If it was, they'd probably use a different verb for it! And parenting *definitely* isn't easy. Like the heroine in this book, I also have a thirteen-year-old son. (I don't have small twins like the hero, but since my kids are only a year apart, they were often mistaken for twins in their preschool years.) The thing about love—and parenting—is that the hard work can yield amazing rewards.

Kate Sullivan loves her son, but he's become increasingly rebellious in the two years since her police officer husband was killed in the line of duty. After a school suspension, Kate decides to take drastic measures and move them to Cupid's Bow, Texas. Kate hopes the fresh start will benefit both her and her son.

But is there room in that fresh start for falling in love?

Sheriff Cole Trent is a single dad with twin five-year-olds. He has his hands full and, much to his match-making mother's chagrin, has declared himself too busy to date. But then he meets Kate Sullivan, a beautiful woman who understands his parenting woes and makes him smile. Their attraction is instant, their chemistry unmistakable. But after the devastating loss of her husband, Kate can't imagine making her heart vulnerable again—especially not with another man in law enforcement. Can Cole convince her that the rewards are worth the risk?

This book is my first set in Cupid's Bow, and I hope you'll come back for future stories about other townspeople! Meanwhile, you can learn more about what I'm writing—and what my crazy family is up to—by following me on Twitter @TanyaMichaels.

Happy reading!

Tanya

FALLING FOR THE SHERIFF

—

Tanya Michaels

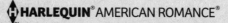
HARLEQUIN® AMERICAN ROMANCE®

Recycling programs
for this product may
not exist in your area.

ISBN-13: 978-0-373-75579-0

Falling for the Sheriff

Copyright © 2015 by Tanya Michna

Printed in U.S.A.

® www.Harlequin.com

Tanya Michaels, a *New York Times* bestselling author and five-time RITA® Award nominee, has been writing love stories since middle school algebra class (which probably explains her math grades). Her books, praised for their poignancy and humor, have received awards from readers and reviewers alike. Tanya is an active member of Romance Writers of America and a frequent public speaker. She lives outside Atlanta with her very supportive husband, two highly imaginative kids and a bichon frise who thinks she's the center of the universe.

Books by Tanya Michaels

Harlequin American Romance

The Best Man in Texas
Texas Baby
His Valentine Surprise
A Mother's Homecoming
"Hill Country Cupid" in *My Cowboy Valentine*

Hill Country Heroes

Claimed by a Cowboy
Tamed by a Texan
Rescued by a Ranger

The Colorado Cades

Her Secret, His Baby
Second Chance Christmas
Her Cowboy Hero

Texas Rodeo Barons

The Texan's Christmas

Visit the Author Profile page
at Harlequin.com for more titles.

This book is dedicated to all my fellow parents out there also raising one of those wondrous and terrifying creatures known as a "teenager."

Prologue

Kate Sullivan had barely spoken on the ride from the middle school to the house. She'd worried that if she opened her mouth to say something, she would start yelling. Or crying. Neither seemed like a good idea while driving.

As they walked in through the garage door that led to the kitchen, her thirteen-year-old son, Luke, broke the tense silence. "I know you're pis—"

"Language!" She spared him a maternal glare over her shoulder.

"I know you're *mad*," he amended. The patronizing emphasis he put on the word was the verbal equivalent of rolling his eyes. "But it really wasn't my fault this time."

Lord, how she wanted to believe him. But the fact that he had to qualify his declaration of innocence with "this time" underscored the severity of his recent behavior problems. As an elementary school music teacher, Kate worked with kids every day. How was it that she could control a roomful of forty students but not her own son? Over the past few months, she'd received phone calls about Luke fighting, lying and cutting classes. And now he'd been suspended!

If Damon were alive…

Her husband, a Houston police officer killed in the line of duty, had been dead for two years. Sometimes, standing here in the familiar red-tiled kitchen, she could still smell the coffee he started every day with, still hear the comforting rumble of his voice. But no amount of wishing him back would change her situation.

She didn't need the imaginary assistance of a ghost. What she needed was a concrete plan. Maybe something radical, because God knew, nothing she'd tried so far had worked, not even the aid of professional therapists.

"It wasn't my knife," Luke continued. "It was Bobby's."

Fourteen-year-old Bobby Rowe and his hard-edged, disrespectful peers were part of the problem.

"Which I *tried* to tell the jackass principal."

Kate slammed her hand down on the counter. "You will not talk about people like that! And you aren't going back to that school." It was a spur of the moment declaration, fraught with logistical complications—she could hardly homeschool and keep her job at the same time—but the minute she heard the words out loud, she knew deep down that a new environment was the right call. She had to get him away from kids like Bobby and away from teachers who were predisposed to believe the worst of Luke because of his recent history.

"Not going back?" His golden-brown eyes widened. He'd inherited what Damon used to call her "lioness coloring," tawny blond hair and amber eyes. "I only got suspended for two days. I can't miss the last three weeks of school."

"Maybe not," she conceded, "but I don't have to send you back there next fall."

"But it's my last year before high school. All my friends are there!"

"You'll make new ones. Non-knife-wielding friends."

"You're really going to send me somewhere different for eighth grade just because you don't like Bobby?"

No, kid, this is because I don't like you—at least, not the person he was on the path to becoming. She loved her son, but on the worst days, she wanted to shake this angry stranger's shoulders and demand to know what he'd done with her generous-natured, artistic Luke.

"I won't get in trouble for the rest of the school year," he vowed desperately.

"Good. But that won't change my mind." She glanced around the kitchen with new eyes. Maybe they could both use a fresh start, more than just a school transfer. She'd stayed in this house after Damon was shot because Luke had suffered such a jarring loss; she hadn't wanted to yank him away from his home and friends. Yet, within six months, he'd found an entirely different group of friends anyway. He no longer associated with the kids who'd known the Sullivans as a whole and intact family. "We're moving."

"*What?* Houston is our home. This was Dad's home! He wouldn't want us to leave."

"He'd want me to do whatever is best for you." And Damon would have wanted her to have help. She wasn't too proud to admit she needed some.

Her father, a professor at the University of Houston's anthropology department, was sweet in a detached, absent way, but he was better with ancient civilizations than living people. Damon's parents adored her, but they'd retired to an active senior community in Florida a year before their son was killed. Since she and Damon had both been only children, that left her with just one other close relative. *Gram.* Affection and a sense of peace she hadn't felt in a long time warmed her.

She closed her eyes, breathing in the memory of summers past. When her father had gone on digs between semesters, she'd stayed with Gram and Grandpa on their small farm. Those idyllic months in the town of Cupid's Bow, Texas, had soothed her soul. Chasing fireflies, tending tomatoes in the garden, fishing in the pond, helping make homemade ice cream to put on Gram's award-winning apple pie...

Although Grandpa had died last year, Gram was still in Cupid's Bow and as feisty as ever. She'd mentioned, though, that it was becoming more difficult to take care of the place by herself and frequently complained that she didn't get to see enough of Kate and Luke. What if they moved in with her? It could benefit all three of them.

Or maybe it would be a horrible idea.

Kate had to try, though. If things didn't change, she could too easily imagine Luke growing into the same kind of thug who'd killed his father. It was time for drastic action.

Cupid's Bow, here we come.

Chapter One

When Sheriff Cole Trent walked into his house the second Saturday of June, he was met in the living room by three irate females. It was only six in the evening, but from the looks he was getting, one would think he'd been out all night. Mirroring their grandmother, his five-year-old twins had their hands on their slim hips and their lips pursed. The family resemblance was unmistakable, although the girls were blonde like the mother who'd run out on them instead of dark-haired like Gayle and Cole.

He sighed. "I know I'm a little later than anticipated, but—"

"A *lot* late," Mandy corrected.

Alyssa's blue eyes were watery. "You promised to take us swimming."

"I didn't promise. I said I'd try." Lately, not even trying his hardest seemed like enough. Once the girls had started kindergarten, they'd become hyperaware that they didn't have a mommy like most of their classmates. Last month's Mother Day had been particularly rough. "Maybe we can go to the pool tomorrow. For now, how about I take you out for barbecue?" He made the offer not just to appease the girls but because he was too worn out to cook.

After a morning testifying in county court and an afternoon of mind-numbing paperwork, Cole's plans to get home early were derailed by the Breelan brothers, three hotheads who never should have gone into business together. The shopkeeper who worked next to their garage had called Cole with a complaint that the Breelans were trying to kill each other. After throwing a few punches—and an impact wrench—Larry Breelan was spending the night in a cell. Deputy Thomas was on duty to make sure neither of Larry's younger brothers tried to bust him out. Or tried to sneak in and murder him, depending on their mood.

Gayle Trent shook her head. "Out to eat again? When was the last time these poor girls had a home-cooked meal?"

Lifelong respect for his mother kept him from rolling his eyes at her dramatic tone, but just barely. "I made them fruit-face pancakes for breakfast. And two nights ago we had dinner at your house. With Jace and William," he reminded her. She'd spent so much conversational energy trying to fix up Cole with various single women that she might not have noticed his brothers were even there.

She continued as if he hadn't spoken. "Speaking of home-cooked meals… Do you remember my friend Joan who owns the little farm down by Whippoorwill Creek? We're in quilting club together and she's signed up to help me inventory donations for the festival auction." The four-day Watermelon Festival every July was one of the town's biggest annual events.

Cole had an uneasy feeling in the pit of his stomach. From the gleam in his mother's eye, she clearly wanted something, and he doubted it was for him to donate an item to auction.

He cleared his throat. "Girls, why don't you go brush your hair and find your shoes so we can leave?" As they scampered off to the far-flung corners of the house to search for the shoes that were always mysteriously disappearing, he returned his attention to his mother, as wary as if he were investigating suspicious noises in a dark alley. "So, what's this about your friend Joan?"

"Her granddaughter, who used to summer here as a kid, is moving to Cupid's Bow with her son. We thought it would be neighborly if you and the girls joined us at the farm for a nice Sunday dinner tomorrow. Joan's inviting other people, too. It's a welcome party," she added, "not a romantic setup."

"Would you swear to that during a polygraph test?"

"Are you calling your own mother a liar?" she asked, looking highly wounded while evading his question. "Not everything is about your love life, you know. Joan's great-grandson won't have many chances to meet kids until school starts again in the fall. I'm sure he'd love to meet the girls. And they'd have fun, too. They were bored silly cooped up in the house with me all afternoon. Joan's farm is like a petting zoo."

"Mom, I—"

The cordless phone on the end table rang, temporarily cutting off his words. Gayle glanced at the display, then smirked in his direction. "Becca Johnston."

His stomach sank at mention of the PTA president who'd been relentlessly pursuing him since her divorce was finalized. "Tell her I'm not here."

"And I can also tell Joan you'll be there for the dinner party tomorrow?" Without waiting for his response, she picked up the phone. "Hello? Oh, hi, Becca." She paused pointedly, one eyebrow raised.

Later, he and his mom were going to discuss the laws prohibiting extortion. For now, he gave a sharp nod, exiting the room to change into civilian clothes and get his girls out of there before his mother talked him into anything else.

Behind him, he heard Gayle say, "Sorry, dear. You just missed him."

"WE'RE GOING TO live *out here*?" Luke's voice reverberated with horror as he stared through the passenger window.

The movie he'd been watching on his tablet had ended a few minutes ago and he seemed to be truly registering their surroundings for the first time. During the peaceful stretch when he'd had his earbuds in, Kate had taken the opportunity to remind herself of all the reasons this relocation was going to be wonderful for them. Sure, Kate didn't have a job yet—and Cupid's Bow Elementary wasn't exactly a rapidly growing school—but she still had paychecks coming through the summer. She could give voice lessons or piano lessons if she got Gram's old upright tuned.

"Yep." She smiled at the picturesque pastures and blue skies. It was after six o'clock, but the June sun was shining brightly. "No traffic, no constant city construction—"

"No internet connection, no cell phone reception," Luke predicted.

"That's not true. Last time I visited Gram, I used my cell phone." She didn't volunteer the information that she'd had to stand with one foot in the laundry room and the other on the attached porch, leaning forty-five degrees to the left while holding on to the dryer. Maybe service had improved since then.

"This is the middle of nowhere! Nobody could possibly live here."

She jerked a thumb toward the side of the road. "The mailboxes suggest otherwise." She appreciated that the mailboxes they'd passed were spread out at roomy intervals. They'd had a nice enough home in the suburbs, but the yards were so small that when Damon used to throw a football with Luke, they spent half their time knocking on the neighbor's door to retrieve the ball from the fenced backyard.

"You're going to love it here," she told Luke. "Lots of community spirit and camaraderie, plenty of home-cooking and fresh air."

He rolled down his window, inhaled deeply, then grimaced. "The fresh air smells like cow poop."

She ground her teeth, refusing to let him spoil her mood. *He'll come around with time.* Her first victory might even be as soon as tonight. Gram could cook like nobody's business, and Luke was a growing boy. A couple of helpings of chicken-fried steak or slow-cooked brisket should improve his outlook on life.

They'd be at the farm in twenty minutes. As eager as Kate was to get there, when she spotted the gas station down the road—the last one before Gram's place—she knew she should stop. The fuel gauge was dropping perilously close to E. Plus, it might be good for her and Luke to get out of the car and stretch their legs for a few minutes.

While she pumped gas, Luke disappeared inside to use the restroom. Although she'd lived her entire life in Texas, sometimes the heat still caught Kate by surprise. Even in the shade, she broke a sweat. She tugged at the lightweight material of her sleeveless blouse to keep it from sticking to her damp skin, then lifted her hair away from her neck, making a mental note to look for an elastic band when she got back in the car.

While waiting for Luke, she went into the station and bought a couple of cold beverages. She'd barely pocketed her change before twisting the lid off her chilled bottle of water and taking a long drink. If Luke didn't hurry, she might finish her water and start in on the fountain soda she held in her other hand.

He was taking a long time, and she wouldn't put it past him to stall in a mulish display of rebellion. She turned with the intention of knocking on the door and hurrying him along, but then stopped herself. Half of parenting was picking one's battles. They'd be at Gram's soon, and her grandmother hadn't seen Luke in months. Was this really the right time to antagonize him? She didn't want him arriving at the farm surly and hostile. A smooth first night might prove to all of them that this could work.

Quit hovering, go to the car. She pivoted with renewed purpose. And crashed into a wall that hadn't been there a moment ago. Okay, technically, the wall was a broad-shouldered man at least six inches taller than she. He wore jeans and a white polo shirt—which was a lot less white with Luke's soda running down the front of it.

Kate opened her mouth to apologize but, "dammit!"

was the first word that escaped. A high-pitched giggle snagged her attention, drawing her gaze downward.

Behind the startled-looking man were two blue-eyed little girls. They were dressed so dissimilarly that it took Kate a moment to realize they were identical. One wore a soccer jersey over camo shorts; tangles of white-blond hair hung in her face, and her sneakers looked as if they were about to disintegrate, held together only by an accumulation of dirt. The other girl was wearing a pink dress that tied at the shoulders and a pair of sparkly sandals. Someone had carefully braided her hair, and she carried a small sequined purse.

Great, she'd doused the guy with a sticky soft drink *and* cursed in front of his young, impressionable children. She'd been in town less than an hour and already needed a fresh start for her fresh start.

"I am *so* sorry." She grabbed a handful of napkins off the counter next to the hot dog rotisserie and began frantically dabbing at his chest.

He covered her hand with his. "Let me."

She glanced up, taking a good look at his face for the first time. *Wow.* Like the girls, he had eyes that were as blue as the Texas sky outside, a dramatic contrast to his jet-black hair. And his—

"Mom? What are you doing?"

Perfect. Her son picked now to return, just in time to catch her ogling a total stranger.

Without waiting for an answer, Luke scowled at the man. "Who are you?"

"Cole." The guy had been handsome already. When he smiled, those eyes crinkling at the corners, the barest hint of a dimple softening that granite jaw, he was breathtaking. "Cole Trent."

DESPITE THE EASY, practiced smile that came with being a public official, Cole's mind was racing as he processed the events of the last few minutes. The jarring chill of icy soda, the rarity of finding himself face-to-face with a stranger when he knew almost everyone in Cupid's Bow and, the biggest surprise of all, the jolt of attraction he experienced when he looked into the woman's amber eyes. He couldn't remember the last time he'd had such an instant reaction to someone.

Was his interest visible in his expression? That could explain the waves of hostility rolling off her son as Cole introduced himself.

From behind him, Alyssa's voice broke into his thoughts. "Daddy, can I have a candy bar?"

He turned, shaking his head. "A candy bar will ruin your appetite."

"But I'm hungggrrry." She drew out the word in a nasal whine.

"Which is why I'm taking you to dinner." They'd only stopped because Mandy had insisted she needed to go to the bathroom and couldn't wait another ten minutes to reach the restaurant; apparently, seeing him doused with soda had temporarily distracted her. "If Mandy will—"

"It's not fair!" Alyssa's lower lip trembled. "I didn't get to go swimming like you said. They ran out of the color I needed to finish my picture at art camp. I don't—"

"That's enough," he said firmly.

But Mandy, who could barely agree with her sister on the color of the sky, picked now of all times to demonstrate twin solidarity. She took a step closer to Alyssa. "It's mean you won't let her have a candy bar."

He fought the urge to glance back at the woman with sun-streaked hair and beautiful eyes. Did she think he was inept at handling his own children? "You're supposed to be in the bathroom," he reminded Mandy. "If you'd hurry, we could be on our way to the Smoky Pig by now. But if the two of you don't stop talking back, we're headed straight home. Understand?"

The threat of having to return home and wait for Cole to cook something motivated Mandy. She navigated the tight aisles of chips and road maps in a rush. He returned his gaze to the woman. The gangly boy who'd called her mom had wandered away to refill his soda cup.

"Kids," Cole said sheepishly. "You have days like this?"

"With a teenager?" She laughed, her dark gold eyes warm and understanding. "Try *every* day."

"I keep waiting for single parenting to get easier, but sometimes I question whether I'm making any progress."

She nodded. "Same here."

So, she was single, too? That thought cheered him more than it should. He didn't even know her name. Nonetheless, he grinned broadly.

She returned the smile, but then ducked her gaze to the sodden napkins in her hand. "I, uh, should throw these away." As she walked toward the trash can, he couldn't help but appreciate the fit of her denim shorts.

Quit leering—there are children present. Well, one of his children, anyway. He turned to see if Alyssa had forgiven him yet. In his peripheral vision, he caught the blonde's son pressing a quick finger to his lips as if sharing a secret with Alyssa. The boy quickly dropped his hand and moved away. Alyssa frowned at her purse.

"Sorry again about the soda." The blonde was back, her tone brisk, as if she wanted to put their encounter behind her. "And good luck with the parenting."

Cole hated to let her go. He wanted to know who she was and why she was here. Was she visiting someone in Cupid's Bow or simply passing through on her way elsewhere? Maybe he would have asked if she hadn't seemed so anxious to go. Or if he weren't busy puzzling over Alyssa's strange expression.

"Good luck to you, too," he said.

With a nod, the blonde walked away, holding the door open for her son.

"Can we go now?" Mandy rejoined them, bouncing on the balls of her feet. "I'm starving!"

"Same here." He ruffled her hair, but kept his gaze on his other daughter. "What about you, Alyssa?"

She jerked her gaze up from her purse, a flush staining her cheeks. Even someone without Cole's training in suspicious behavior would have spotted the guilt in her eyes.

"What have you got in your purse?" he asked.

"N-nothing." She clutched the small sequined bag to her body.

He held out his hand, making it clear he wanted to see for himself.

Tears welled in her eyes as she pulled a candy bar from her purse. "B-but I didn't take it! That boy gave me it."

Cole's blood pressure skyrocketed. Alyssa was, by nature, a sweet, quiet girl, but throughout her kindergarten year—after every field trip or class party where other students had mothers present—she'd grown increasingly unpredictable. The teacher who had once praised his daughter's reading skill and eager-to-please disposition had started calling Cole about behavior problems, including a memorable graffiti incident. Now some punk was trying to turn Alyssa into a shoplifter, too? Hell, no.

"HEY!"

Kate jumped at the angry boom, nearly dropping her car keys. She turned to see Cole Trent, the single dad who'd melted her insides with his smile. He wasn't smiling now.

He strode across the parking lot like a man on a mission. One of his daughters was sobbing. The other looked grimly fascinated, as if she'd never expected a simple pit stop to be so eventful.

"Aw, crap." Luke's barely audible words—and the resignation in them—caused Kate's heart to sink.

Not again. Not here! In her mind, she'd built up Cupid's Bow as a safe haven. But how could you escape trouble when it was riding shotgun?

"What did you do?" she demanded in a low voice.

He slouched, not meeting her eyes. "It was only an eighty-nine cent candy bar. Jeez."

Cole reached them in time to hear her son's careless dismissal, his blue eyes bright with righteous fury. "It's more than a candy bar, young man. It's stealing."

Kate's stomach churned. "You *stole*?"

Cole's gaze momentarily softened as he glanced at her, registering her stress. When he spoke again, his tone was calmer. "Perhaps I should reintroduce myself. I'm *Sheriff* Cole Trent. What's your name, son?"

"Luke," he muttered.

"And did you put that candy bar in Alyssa's purse?" the sheriff asked in an unyielding, don't-even-think-about-lying tone.

The boy hunched his shoulders. "I felt bad for her."

Was that even true, Kate wondered, or had her son simply seized an opportunity for petty defiance?

Cole gave his sniffling daughter a stern look. "Luke may have been the one to take the candy bar, but you should have put it back. Or told me what happened. Other people's bad behavior is no excuse for acting badly yourself."

Terrific. Now her son was a cautionary tale for younger children.

"The two of you are going back inside to admit what you did and apologize to Mr. Jacobs," Cole said.

His daughter gulped. The man behind the counter had smiled pleasantly at Kate, but she could see where his towering height, all black clothing and tattooed arms might intimidate a little girl.

"While you're there," Kate told Luke, "ask what you can do to make up for it." He was too young for an official part-time job, but it was clear Kate needed to find ways to keep him busy and out of trouble. "Maybe they could use a volunteer to come by a few times a week and pick up litter in the parking lot."

Cole's gaze swung to her. "A few times a week? So you aren't just passing through or visiting? You're sticking around?"

Was that surprise she heard in his voice, or dread? Given his duty to maintain law and order in the county, he probably didn't relish the idea of a juvenile delinquent moving to town. And Gram deserved better than a great-grandson who caused her problems in the community. Was this experiment doomed to fail?

"We're staying with family in the area. Indefinitely." She forced a smile and tried to sound reassuring. "But I plan to stay out of public until I learn how to properly carry sodas, and Luke may be grounded for the rest of the summer. So you don't have to worry about us menacing the populace, I promise."

The size of Cupid's Bow might make it difficult to avoid someone, but she was willing to try. Between the terrible impression her son had made and Kate's aversion to being around cops since Damon's death, she rather desperately hoped never to see Sheriff Trent again.

Chapter Two

After Luke and his unwitting accomplice apologized to the gruff but fair Mr. Jacobs, Kate and her son resumed their journey. He had the good sense not to resume his complaining.

It wasn't until they were jostling along the private dirt road that led up to Gram's house that Luke spoke again. "Are you going to tell her about the gas station? And the sheriff?"

She sighed. "Well, it wasn't going to be my opening. I thought we'd say hi first and thank her profusely for taking us under her roof before we hit her with news of your exciting new criminal activities."

"I apologized," Luke grumbled. "I even paid the guy, although no one ended up with the candy bar."

"'The guy' is Mr. Jacobs, and you're going to treat him with respect when you see him next weekend." It turned out that the inked man with the gravelly voice visited the pediatric ward of the hospital once a month and gave a magic show. Luke's penance was that he would sacrifice a Saturday morning to work as the man's assistant. "And paying for what you took after the fact doesn't justify what you did. You know better than to steal! Your own father was a policeman, who—"

"My father is gone," he said flatly.

She parked the car, and turned to look at her son. "I miss him, too. And I get angry—at him, at the man who shot him, at the unfairness of life. But lashing out and doing dumb things won't bring your dad back. It only drives a wedge between you and me. I'm still here for you, kiddo. Try to remember that?"

Without responding, he climbed out of the car.

She blinked against the sting of tears, preferring to meet her grandmother with a smile. Joan Denby had lost her husband even more recently than Kate. The two women were supposed to bolster each other, not drag each other further down.

Either Gram had been watching for them, or Patch, the eight-year-old German shepherd, had barked notice of their arrival. Kate had barely removed her seatbelt before Gram hurried out onto the wraparound porch to greet them. In a pair of purple capris and a polo shirt striped with hot pink, Joan Denby was a splash of vivid color against the white wood railing. She looked much the same as she had all those summers when Kate visited as a girl, except that the cloud of once-dark hair framing Gram's face was silver and her lively hazel eyes now peered at the world through a pair of bifocals. Still, few would guess that she was the great-grandmother of a teenager.

"Luke! Katie!" The exuberant welcome in her voice carried on the breeze, and the knot in Kate's stomach unraveled.

Home. Whatever happened during the next few weeks of transition, Kate was suddenly 100 percent certain this was where she was supposed to be. Her vision blurred again, but this time with happy tears. She jumped out of the car, not even bothering to shut the door before rushing to hug her grandmother.

"I've missed you," she whispered fiercely. Even though she now stood taller than the woman who'd been equal parts mom and grandmother to her, Gram's embrace still made Kate feel safer, just as it had when she'd woken from nightmares as a girl or been rattled by a Texas thunderstorm.

"Missed you, too, Katie. So much." Gram patted her on the back, then pulled away to reach for Luke. "And you! I can't believe how tall you're getting. Strong enough to help with farm chores, I reckon. But don't worry," she added with a smile, "I promise to make sure you're well-compensated with your favorite desserts."

"Anything but candy bars," he mumbled.

Kate suppressed a groan at the reminder of their inauspicious entry to town. "We should start bringing in bags," she told her son. "The car's not going to unpack itself."

Gram followed them. "I expected to see you hauling a trailer of stuff."

"We brought most of our personal items, but the furniture's in storage back in Houston." She didn't add that she hadn't wanted to move it all twice in case this relocation didn't work out.

Gram insisted on helping, and Kate gave her the lightest things she could find in the backseat. Kate faltered at the box of Luke's art supplies. It had been sheer optimism on her part to bring them; he'd told her she could leave them in storage—or throw them away.

There'd been a time when he'd never been without a sketch pad of some kind. A few months before Damon was killed, Luke had started working on a comic book series about a superhero on another planet. The interstellar crime-fighter didn't have a family and he'd possessed larger than life mystical powers, but the physical resemblance between Luke's fictional champion and his dad had been unmistakable.

His earlier statement echoed in her mind. *My father is gone.* But he hadn't only lost Damon. In the last two years, he seemed to have also lost his inspiration and his direction. Although there was no need to get the heavy box inside before dinner, she vowed to put the supplies in his room later. Maybe, with time and patience, he'd find his direction again.

Shifting a large satchel against her hip, she pulled a rolling suitcase from the trunk. "Am I in my usual room, Gram?" Even during her trips to the farm as an adult, Kate had stayed in the bedroom where she had so many happy childhood memories.

Her grandmother nodded. "Of course. And for Luke, I cleared out the room where Jim used to work on his model planes. It's not huge, but it's the least girly space in the house."

"I'm sure it will be fine," Kate said gently, hating the thought of Gram boxing up all of her late husband's beloved planes alone. She wished her father was more reliable, that he lived close enough to regularly visit his widowed mother. Not that geography was any guarantee he'd pull his head out of his textbooks long enough to remember his family. The cliché "absent-minded professor" aptly described James Sullivan Jr. The last time he'd had dinner with Kate and Luke, he'd seemed sincerely shocked that his grandson wasn't still nine years old.

Patch met them at the front door with baritone yowls and a tail wagging wildly enough to generate a windstorm. It took a few minutes to get past the excited shepherd and into the living room. Kate took in the familiar surroundings, recalling her grandfather's good-natured complaints about the pink curtains and throw pillows on the sofa. Gram had told him that, if it made him feel better, the color was technically "country rose." He'd also pretended to be annoyed by her collection of carousel-horse figurines, but he'd built her the gorgeous display cabinet that housed them.

The room had barely changed in the last decade. Even the warm, inviting scent was the same. Gram's house always smelled like a combination of the lemony cleaner she used on the hardwood floors and pecan pie.

Luke raised his head, sniffing appreciatively, but it wasn't floor cleaner and nostalgia that captured his interest. "Food!"

Gram laughed. "I have beef stew in the slow-cooker and made a batch of corn bread muffins."

He immediately dropped the large duffel bags, as if preparing to bolt for the kitchen.

"We're not just leaving our stuff all over Gram's house," Kate chided, familiar with his habits. Their home in Houston had often been an obstacle course of discarded tennis shoes, an unzipped backpack with class binders spilling out of it and dirty glasses that should have been carried to the sink. "Once you've got the bags in your room and washed your hands, we'll see about dinner." He must have been genuinely hungry because, rather than flashing one of his mutinous scowls, he dashed down the hallway.

"It's gratifying to cook for someone other than just myself," Gram said, a trace of sadness beneath her smile.

Kate's heart squeezed, but she kept her tone light. "As much food as Luke puts away, you may get tired of it pretty quickly. I insist you let me help with meals. And everything else—cleaning, gardening, whatever needs to be done. I know how seriously you take hospitality, but Luke and I are roommates, not guests who have to be waited on hand and foot."

Gram's eyes twinkled. "Well…now that you mention it, I suppose I could use your help with a welcome party I'm hosting. Tomorrow."

"You planned a party tomorrow?" *So much for settling in slowly.* Kate had hoped to sleep late, then spend the day unpacking.

"*Party* is probably too grandiose a term. It's just a neighborhood cookout. I invited some friends, like the Rosses, who live down the road. You remember they used to let you ride their horses? And I figured you'd want to see Crystal Tucker. Wait—she's Crystal Walsh now, isn't she?" Gram shook her head. "Seems like just yesterday the two of you were sharing cotton candy at the Watermelon Festival, a couple of kids with pigtails and sticky hands. Now you're all grown up with kids of your own!"

Kate and Crystal had bonded quickly after meeting at the community pool and renewed their friendship every summer. An only child, Kate had loved having a playmate in town. Crystal, the middle kid between two sisters, relished the comparative peace and quiet at the Denby farm. The last time they'd seen each other was Jim Denby's funeral, but Crystal, heavily pregnant with twin boys, hadn't been able to stay long. It would be nice to catch up with her. Kate tried to recall the age of Crystal's oldest son, hoping the boy could be a potential friend for Luke. He needed a wholesome peer group—the sooner, the better.

With that goal in mind, she gave her grandmother a grateful smile. "I hate for you to go to trouble on our account, but I'm really glad you're throwing the welcome party. I'm sure it will be exactly what we need."

KATE WAS GLAD her son had the good sense not to show up at the dinner table wearing earbuds—a mandate she'd had to repeat at least once a week back in Houston—but he wasn't the most effusive dinner companion. He wolfed down two servings of stew while barely looking up from his plate, then asked to be excused.

She sighed, wishing he showed more curiosity about their new surroundings and learning about Cupid's Bow. *Let him go.* It had been a long day, and no doubt tomorrow would bring fresh battles. "You're excused, but make sure you rinse your dishes."

He did as asked, then paused in the doorway that led to the hall. "Dinner was awesome," he mumbled in Gram's general direction, the words all strung together. Then he disappeared around the corner.

Kate shook her head. "Well, that was a start, I guess. We'll work on eye contact later."

Gram smiled. "He's had a tough time of it. You both have."

"I know." Lord, did she know. "But that doesn't give him a permanent get-out-of-jail-free card. Losing his dad can't become a habitual excuse for bad choices." She ran a hand through her hair, recalling the incident at the gas station. She'd meant get-out-of-jail in a figurative sense, but if her son didn't get off his current path…

"Katie?" Gram's tone was thick with concern.

Glancing toward the empty doorway, Kate lowered her voice. "We had a mishap on the way to the farm… and by *mishap*, I mean petty larceny. He stole from Rick Jacobs, got caught shoplifting a candy bar at the gas station. Luke didn't even want it. We'd been arguing in the car and I can't help feeling like this was another act of rebellion because he's mad at me. He took the candy bar for a little girl."

Kate covered her eyes, her face heating at the mortifying memory. "He got busted stealing candy for one of Cole Trent's daughters."

"He stole something for the *sheriff's* kid?" Gram made an odd noise that Kate belatedly identified as a snort of amusement.

"Gram! It's not funny."

"It sort of is. Cupid's Bow is small, granted, but there are a couple thousand residents. Of all the people…" She tried unsuccessfully to smother another laugh. "The sheriff! Seriously?"

"Trust me, I wouldn't joke about this. When we met him inside, we didn't know he was a cop. Then he chased us out in the parking lot, understandably furious. I was so embarrassed." And that was after she'd already enjoyed the super-fun humiliation of dumping her drink on him. "Frankly, I'm hoping to avoid Sheriff Trent for the next three or four…ever."

Gram's eyes widened. "Oh, but—surely your paths

will cross again. Like I said, this is a small town. So, perhaps it would be best to get it over with sooner rather than later. Right?"

Definitely not. But since it seemed rude to argue, Kate smiled weakly. "I suppose that's one way of looking at it." Another way to view it was that Kate had enough on her plate already without worrying about alienating a blue-eyed pillar of the community.

CRAP. LUKE SULLIVAN scowled at the prolonged quiet on the other side of the bedroom door. *They're talking about me.* He couldn't make out any of his mom's or great-grandmother's words, but he knew the tense, muffled tone. His mother had used it with his therapist whenever she sent Luke out of the room so the two adults could confer privately. She'd used it a lot on the phone with her friends when she was complaining about Luke's screw-ups.

Suddenly needing noise and lots of it, Luke shoved in his earbuds and cranked up the volume on a hip-hop song. It was enough to drown out the low drone of conversation in the kitchen, but it didn't mute the thoughts bouncing around his brain. He didn't want to be here, in this shoebox of a room that smelled faintly of paint fumes. He liked his great-grandmother, but this was *her* house, not his. He missed home.

And he missed his friends.

He knew his mom didn't like them, had specifically heard her describe Bobby as a "hoodlum," but she didn't get it. When he hung out with Bobby and the other eighth graders, kids looked at him with respect. Bobby was a known badass. He wasn't universally liked, but even being regarded with contempt was better than pity. Luke hated students and teachers and neighbors eyeing him like he was a pathetic baby bird who'd fallen out of its nest and effed up its wing.

He was sick of people asking if he was "okay," like his father's murder was something to get over, equal to bombing a math quiz. He was tired of his mom's stubborn attempts to get him to hang out with his old friends. And her attempts to get him to draw again. What did she care? Comic books were dumb stories that had nothing to do with real life.

In the stories Luke used to doodle, his cyborg-enhanced alien helped people by stopping natural disasters and chasing off enemies. In real life, Luke couldn't even help cheer up a little girl. Stealing the candy had been stupid, and he certainly hadn't meant to get her in trouble. He hated seeing girls cry.

He knew his mom cried. After his dad got shot, she'd cried a lot. They both had. But then she'd pretended to stop. He wasn't stupid, though. He noticed when her face was blotchy. Some nights when he couldn't sleep, he could hear the muffled noise. He hated those nights. He hated that his dad had picked such a dangerous job. He hated that he'd had to leave the only place he'd ever lived. But there wasn't anything Luke could *do* about those problems.

Frustration flooded him, and he clenched his fists.

Yeah, stealing the candy bar had been a dumbass thing to do but it had seemed like such a simple solution, an easy way to make that little girl stop crying. Finally, there'd been a problem that seemed fixable! But he hadn't been able even to fix that. So how was he going to fix the rest of his life?

AFTER THE ACHES and pains caused by loading the car and hours of driving, Kate expected to toss and turn all night. Instead, only a few minutes after her head hit the pillow, she fell into a dreamless sleep. In the morning, she woke to a wave of déjà vu triggered by the scent of coffee. She herself had never developed a taste for it, but Damon hadn't been able to form the words *good morning* without a mug in his hand.

To combat the Texas summer, Gram kept the air-conditioning chugging at a temperature low enough to cool the hardwood floors. Kate slid her feet into music-note slippers given to her by a student at Christmas and padded to the kitchen to help with breakfast. She wasn't surprised that the door to Luke's room was still closed; he rarely got out of bed without parental prompting.

Gram, a natural morning person, beamed at her. "Sleep well, dear?"

"Like a rock, actually." It was the best night's rest she'd had in recent memory.

"I was just about to scramble myself some eggs. Want some?"

"You made dinner last night. It only seems fair that I make breakfast," Kate counteroffered.

"All right. Then I can work on my shopping list. I'm running into town to pick up a few last minute items for the cookout this afternoon."

The two women ate breakfast in companionable silence. Afterward, Gram gathered her purse and keys, saying she wouldn't be gone long. She was just missing a few ingredients for the desserts she planned to bake.

Alone in the quiet house, Kate began unpacking some of her belongings into the closet and bureau. She'd been too drained last night. After making a substantial dent—and finding a casual green-striped sundress that seemed appropriate for today—she headed for the bathroom and showered. She used the blow-dryer with the door open, hoping the noise would jump-start the process of waking Luke. When she knocked on his door, however, there was no answer, not even a mumbled "go away."

She toyed with letting him sleep longer, wondering if that would improve his disposition today, but decided she wanted this opportunity while they were alone in the house to break the news about the welcome party. He might not react with enthusiasm, and she didn't want him hurting Gram's feelings.

"Knock, knock," she said as she pushed the door open.

He was out cold, his breathing slow and even, his shaggy hair going in all different directions, an uneven halo against the pale blue pillowcase. Without the scowl that was rapidly becoming his trademark, he looked a lot like he had as a little boy. Her heart constricted, a tight ball in her chest. She loved her son so much and wanted nothing more than to make his life better, easier. If only he could see that!

She sat on the edge of the bed, saying his name softly, then with more volume, jostling his shoulder.

One eyelid cracked open just enough for him to peer at her in displeasure. "Whaddayawant?"

"To make you breakfast. And to talk. We saved you some bacon," she said coaxingly.

He hesitated, torn between two of his favorite activities—sleeping and eating. Playing video games was also in his top five, but she hadn't hooked up his gaming system last night. Maybe that could be his reward for being well-behaved today.

"Why don't you put on some clothes and brush your teeth," she suggested, "and I'll cook you some eggs. Scrambled with cheese?"

He shook his head. "Fried with the squishy yolk, so that the yellow runs everywhere when you cut it."

"Okay." She rose, leaving the room and giving him some privacy. But she hesitated in the hallway, listening to make sure he actually got out of the bed instead of rolling over and falling back to sleep.

Just as she was setting his plate on the table, he appeared in the kitchen, wearing a pair of maroon shorts with an elastic waist and a charcoal-colored shirt that had once featured the name of a sports team. The letters had faded to obscurity after about a million washings, and tiny holes in the fabric were beginning to appear at the neckline and around the seams. He claimed the shirt was the softest piece of clothing he owned and wore it about three times a week. She really needed to find him a replacement before this one ultimately disintegrated. Although he'd changed, he hadn't taken the time to brush his hair. It stuck out around his face in fluffy spikes.

She handed him a glass of orange juice. "You sleep okay?" Considering the coma-like condition she'd found him in, it seemed like a safe opener.

"No. The bed's lumpy, and the outside noise is weird."

How did he not consider the gentle hum of crickets and tree frogs an improvement over planes landing and periodic car alarms blaring? "There's hardly any noise at all!"

"That's what makes it weird." He stabbed into an egg, watching the yellow ooze across the plate as requested. "Where's Gram?"

"She went out for some groceries." And would probably be home any minute now, so Kate better get to the point. "She invited some people over this afternoon for a cookout."

Luke scowled around a mouthful of bacon. "You want me to spend my afternoon with a bunch of people I don't know?"

"That's the whole point of the gathering, so we can get to know some of our new neighbors. Maybe start making friends."

"I *have* friends. In Houston."

"Well, we aren't in Houston anymore. Gram was nice enough to take us in, and we owe her. Our actions here reflect on her, too."

"So you're saying if we don't fit in, she might kick us out?"

"Of course not!" Her grandmother would never resort to reverse extortion. Was he asking because he feared not being accepted, after the way most of his teachers had labeled him last year, or was he secretly hopeful, wondering if antics at Gram's cookout could be his ticket back to Houston?

"I expect you to be on your *best* behavior," she stressed. "Do not screw this up."

Hurt flared in his eyes, but his tone was his default-mode sarcastic when he said, "So you're saying I *shouldn't* hotwire the guests' cars and do doughnuts in the back pasture?"

"After your stunt yesterday, you don't get to make jokes like that."

"How long are you going to stay mad about that? It was just a stupid candy bar!"

No, it was a destructive pattern of behavior. Then again, if she always acted as though she expected the worst of him, was she creating a self-fulfilling prophecy? "Luke, I—"

Outside, a car door closed, and he shot out of his chair. "I'll see if she needs help bringing in groceries." His gallantry was clearly motivated by an excuse to end the conversation, but Kate would take what she could get.

The screen door clattered as he hurried out of the house, and Kate heard Gram call good morning to him. Decades ago, Joan Denby had been able to coax Kate out of her shell when she was feeling abandoned by her father. Maybe now Gram could work her magic on a sullen teenage boy.

There were so few bags that Luke got them all in one trip. Kate offered to help put away the groceries, but Gram said to just leave them out for baking. She then made Luke's day by giving him permission to hook up his game console to the living room TV while the two women worked in the kitchen.

Once he'd happily scampered off to lose himself in a digital quest, Gram raised an eyebrow in Kate's direction. "Am I wrong, or was there some tension between the two of you?"

"Always."

Gram patted her arm. "Hang in there. The teen years are difficult. I seem to recall a certain summer where you and Crystal fell for the same lifeguard at the local pool and life as you knew it was *over*!" She pressed the back of her hand to her forehead in melodramatic parody.

Kate chuckled in spite of herself. "Okay, I suppose even I had my tantrums."

"And you grew into a wonderful woman. Luke has a good heart."

"I know. I just wish he'd share it with people more often."

Gram disappeared into the walk-in pantry and returned with a sack of flour and an armful of spices. "Do you want an apron to protect your dress? It's pretty. Brings out the green in your eyes." She beamed proudly. "You're sure to make a good impression in it."

Alarm bells sounded in Kate's head, as jarring as a classroom of seven-year-olds all playing xylophones for the first time. Suddenly she recalled a phone conversation with Gram a few months ago. Her grandmother had gently hinted that Luke might do better with a male role model in his life and asked if Kate ever dated. When Kate had said no, Gram had dropped the subject. Now, Kate wondered if her grandmother had simply been biding her time.

"Gram, this welcome party... It's not going to be a lineup of the county's eligible bachelors, is it? I told you, I'm not ready for romance."

Her grandmother smiled sadly. "I lost my husband, too. I understand. But you're in the prime of your life, with a lot of years left ahead of you. Damon wouldn't want you to be alone."

That answer did nothing to settle Kate's apprehension about the party. "Today isn't going to be you, me, and a dozen single guys between the ages of twenty and fifty, right?"

"You have your grandfather's active imagination. As I told you last night, I invited some families. Now, can we get started? I've got several desserts I want to bake, and my oven will only hold so many things at a time."

Telling herself to quit being paranoid, Kate lost herself in the comforting rhythm of working alongside the woman who had taught her how to cook. The first dinner she'd ever fixed for Damon had included her grandmother's chicken and dumplings recipe. The hours passed quickly. In seemingly no time, afternoon sun streamed through the windows and the kitchen smelled like a decadent bakery. Unfortunately, the kitchen was nearly as hot as the inside of a bakery oven.

At least outside there was a breeze. Kate covered long folding tables with vinyl tablecloths, glad she hadn't bothered with makeup. It would have melted away. They drafted Luke to dump ice into the drink coolers and pretended not to notice all the food he stole off the veggie tray. Beans simmered on the stove, and a vat of potato salad waited in the fridge. The smell of brisket cooking made Kate's stomach rumble. While she waited for the grill to heat up so she could throw on some sausages, she opened a bag of tortilla chips and taste-tested Gram's homemade salsa.

Gram handed her a cold water bottle, her eyes glinting with mischief. "You might want this."

Kate nodded. "It's a little hotter than I remembered."

"Well. Everyone needs a little spice in their lives."

As Kate sipped her water, two vehicles came down the dirt road that led from the street to the farm. The second was a battered pickup; the one in the lead was a sedan that was probably older than she was but gleamed as if it were washed and waxed daily. As soon as it pulled to a stop, the back door opened. While the driver and front passenger were still dealing with their seatbelts, two blonde blurs of energy spilled out. Followed by a tall man with ink-black hair.

Cold water splashed over her fingers, making her realize she was squeezing the bottle in her hand. "Gram!" She couldn't keep the note of shrill accusation from her voice. "That is Cole Trent."

Her grandmother ducked her gaze. "Oh. Did I, um, forget to mention he was invited?"

Chapter Three

A single glance across the shaded front yard confirmed the suspicion that had been growing inside Cole as his father drove. Joan Denby's granddaughter was indeed the beautiful blonde he'd met yesterday. Two single moms with sons moving to Cupid's Bow at the same time wasn't impossible, but it would be an unlikely coincidence. When the possibility had first occurred to him that the woman they were welcoming to town was the same one he'd met at the gas station, he'd discounted it because his mother had made it sound as if the newcomer's son was closer to the twins' age.

Then again, his mom had proven that her ethics were flexible when it came to introducing him to single women.

He had to admit, on some level, he was excited to see the blonde again. Judging from her tense body language as she talked to her grandmother, the feeling was not mutual.

"Hey, it's that lady!" Mandy announced as the adults unloaded folding chairs and covered dishes from the car.

Gayle Trent glanced at her granddaughter. "The older one, or the younger one?"

Mandy frowned, momentarily perplexed that some-one over thirty might qualify as young. "The one with the ponytail. We met her yesterday. Her son's a big kid. He and Alyssa took a—"

"I *didn't* take it!" Alyssa interrupted, her face splotched with red.

"Why don't we leave what happened in the past?" Cole said, steering his girls away from his mother's bla-tant curiosity. He had not yet shared the Great Candy Bar Heist with her. "Come on, let's go meet our host-ess."

He tried to recall whether his mom had mentioned Joan's granddaughter by name but drew a blank.

"Sheriff Trent!" Joan Denby waved him over with a smile. "So nice to see you—and your girls. They're getting so big. This is my granddaughter, Kate Sulli-van. I hear the two of you have met?"

"Briefly, but I didn't catch a name." He set down the chairs he carried and extended his hand. "Nice to officially meet you, Kate."

Her gold-green eyes narrowed and, for a second, he didn't think she would shake his hand. She did, but the contact was as fleeting as social protocol allowed.

"Sheriff," she said stiffly.

He smiled. "Please, call me Cole. I'm off duty at the moment."

His parents had caught up to them and Mr. and Mrs. Ross, who owned The Twisted R ranch at the end of the road, were climbing down from their truck and calling their own hellos. Cole stepped out of the way, giving Joan a chance to proudly introduce her granddaugh-ter. As Kate greeted everyone, her gaze kept darting nervously back to him. The lingering interest would be flattering if not for her apprehensive expression.

He was used to being well-regarded in the community and frankly unsure how to respond to her thinned lips and rigid posture. Did she somehow blame him for her son's actions yesterday? After all, if his daughter hadn't asked for the candy bar in the first place, Luke might never have swiped it. She certainly hadn't made excuses for her son, though. She'd responded to the situation with a directness Cole admired, marching her son back inside to apologize to Rick Jacobs and offer restitution.

"Mom!" The front door banged open, releasing an exuberant German shepherd into the yard. Luke Sullivan emerged on the wraparound porch. "There's some lady on the phone for you."

At the sight of Luke, Alyssa gasped. Apparently, it hadn't yet clicked with her that if Kate was present, her son would be, too. "I do not like him," Alyssa said to no one in particular before stomping off to sit beneath a pear tree.

Mandy watched her sister's retreat with wide eyes, then tugged Cole's hand. "Now what?"

Good question.

"Of course I understand," Kate said into the phone, trying to concentrate on Crystal's words instead of staring at the sheriff through the front window. "We'll get together for lunch or something as soon as everyone's feeling better."

Her childhood friend had called with the news that two of her kids had the stomach flu. When the first one had thrown up, Crystal had hoped it was an isolated incident and had planned to leave her husband at home with the kid. But now that there were fevers involved, Crystal worried that even the members of the household not showing symptoms might be contagious.

"I can't wait to see you," Crystal said, her tone apologetic. "I hate that I won't make the barbecue."

"Me, too." Catching up with her old friend would have been a nice distraction from Sheriff Trent. *Call me Cole.* His rich voice was more tempting than Gram's desserts. "Hey, Crys, do you know much about the sheriff? Gram invited him and his parents."

"Then she has good taste," Crystal said approvingly. "He's a cutie."

Cute did not begin to describe him. The casual cotton T-shirt he wore delineated his muscular arms and chest far more than the crisp polo shirt she'd last seen on him. And she felt foolish for noticing that in the full sunlight, his thick hair wasn't simply black. Half a dozen subtler hues threaded through it.

She was not interested in the sheriff's hair. Or his muscles. Mostly, she just wanted to make sure Luke behaved today and didn't further damage his reputation with the sheriff—or any of the other guests, for that matter.

"One of my boys played soccer in the spring with Mandy Trent," Crystal said. "The sheriff's got his hands full, but he seems like a good dad. And he's considered quite the catch among the women in town. Or would be, if anyone could catch him."

"So he's not seeing anyone?" Kate wished she could take back the impulsive question. The sheriff's dating life was none of her concern.

"I don't think he's gone on more than three dates

with the same woman since his divorce, which was years ago. Popular opinion is that Becca Johnston will wear him down eventually—unless he gets a restraining order. Becca's relentless, never takes no for an answer. Every time she calls, I get sandbagged into chairing some PTA committee or local food drive. If you want to volunteer for something like the Watermelon Festival in order to meet people, you should talk to her. If not, avoid her like the plague. And speaking of plague, I'd better go check my sick kids."

As Kate was replacing the cordless phone on its charger, the front door opened.

"Katie?" Gram's tone was rueful. No doubt she felt guilty for the way she'd ambushed Kate with Cole's presence. "Are you rejoining us?"

Like I have a choice? "You raised me better than to hide in the house just because there's someone I'd rather avoid. I was talking to Crystal. She had to cancel because they're dealing with a stomach bug."

"I'm sorry to hear that. She was excited about seeing you again."

Kate shrugged, trying not to look as disappointed as she felt. "Sick kids come with the parenting territory. I'll see her soon."

"You know, I thought there was a chance Cole might have to cancel," Gram said. "As sheriff, he's got a lot of responsibilities. Just keeping the Breelan brothers under control is practically a full-time job. As fretful as you were about seeing him again, it seemed unkind to worry you needlessly in the event he couldn't make it."

"As opposed to giving me time to mentally prepare myself?"

"Well…we did both agree that it would be best for

you to encounter him sooner rather than later," Gram said, taking some creative license with the conversation they'd actually had. "Please don't be angry. His mother is a close friend. Your paths were bound to cross. Give him a chance."

A chance to what? "I'm not angry, Gram. You invited his family before you knew Cole and I had shared an awkward run-in. I'm sure he's a nice man. But, at the risk of being repetitive, I really don't—"

"Oh, I just remembered! I need to stir the beans so they don't burn on the bottom. Excuse me, dear." Gram moved with impressive speed for a woman over seventy. "Will you let our guests know I'll be back in a moment?"

"For the record," Kate grumbled with wry amusement, "I know perfectly well I'm being manipulated."

Gram flashed a cheeky smile over her shoulder. One thing was for sure, living with a crafty grandmother and an unpredictable teen would keep Kate on her toes.

LUKE JAMMED HIS hands in the pockets of his cargo shorts, wishing he could disappear. With his mom and Gram both inside the house, he didn't know any of the other adults. Except the sheriff—and Luke would rather not face him.

One of the sheriff's daughters was pleading with her dad to kick a soccer ball back and forth; the other girl had gone off by herself. In Luke's opinion, she had the right idea. He suddenly found himself walking in that direction.

Although the twins were technically identical, they were pretty easy to tell apart. The one beneath the tree had a pink backpack and her hair was braided the same way it had been yesterday; she was the one who'd wanted the candy bar. Alyssa, her dad had called her.

She glared when she saw him coming. "I don't like you."

A common opinion. Luke wasn't sure his mom liked him, either. Sometimes, he wasn't even sure he liked himself. "Whatcha got there?"

"Nothing." She hunched forward, protectively. He couldn't see what she was drawing, but he could tell she had a sketch pad in her lap. Crayons spilled from her open backpack across the grass.

"What are you drawing?"

"Go away."

The side of his mouth lifted in a grin. For a little kid, she certainly wasn't intimidated by a teenager twice her height. "I didn't mean to get you in trouble yesterday." Despite the way his stomach had hurt when he'd seen the Trents in the yard, now he was kind of glad they were here. The chance to apologize was an unexpected relief. "I'm sorry. Really."

Her head lifted, and she studied him for a long moment.

"I was just trying to do something nice," he added. "I thought he should have bought you the candy bar."

"You made a poor decision." The way she said it sounded like she was imitating an adult. Her dad, probably.

Jealousy pinched Luke's insides. It caught him off guard whenever he felt this—envy for all the regular kids who still had fathers. It wasn't as if he wanted anyone else's dad to die. He just wished his own was still around. Sometimes Luke could hear his dad's voice so clearly he could almost pretend they were on the phone.

Other days, his dad's voice was faded and distorted, like bad audio on a corrupt game file.

His throat burning, he backed away from Alyssa. "I'll leave you alone."

"Wait! It's a horse." She held up the pad. "But it's not very good."

It was terrible. The legs weren't the right scale to the rest of the body, the neck was weirdly lumpy, and the nose looked like a crocodile snout. Plus, horses shouldn't be purple. But he didn't want to hurt her feelings. What if she cried again?

"Keep trying. With enough practice, you could get so good you surprise yourself." He'd heard his mom say that to music students. He hoped it would be enough to make Alyssa feel better about her mutant horse. He stared at the picture, trying to find a positive. "The tail looks right."

"Thank you." She brightened a little. "My nana said this is a farm. Do you have horses?"

"No. There are goats, though." Taking her toward the barn to look for the goats would kill some time until the food was ready *and* keep Luke away from the sheriff. "Wanna go see them?"

"Okay." She picked up her backpack, frowning as she zipped it. "But don't you dare stick candy in my bag."

He recalled his mom's stern warning. *Do not screw this up.* Everyone thought he was too stupid to learn from his mistakes. "I said I was sorry."

"Then I guess you can be my friend."

"Gee, thanks." His first friend in a new town, and it was a five-year-old girl. Still, as they headed to the barn, he had to admit it was kind of nice not to be walking alone.

COLE HAD JUST retrieved the soccer ball from some rose bushes at the side of the house when his dad clapped him on the back.

"You look like you could use a break, son." Harvey Trent said. "Mandy, I'm not sure your dad can keep up with you! How about Paw-paw takes a turn while your dad grabs a cold drink?" Lowering his voice to a whisper, he added, "And talks to the pretty girl."

Cole groaned. "Did Mom put you up to this?"

Harvey took the soccer ball from his son's hands. "No one has to 'put me up to' enjoying time with my granddaughter."

If Cole's parents thought Kate Sullivan wanted him to talk to her, they must be blind. The woman's "stay back" vibe was so strong, he expected to see gnats and butterflies bouncing off the invisible force field that surrounded her. After the casseroles other women in town had baked him over the years and Becca Johnston's less than subtle pursuit, Kate's disinterest should be refreshing. Except…he wouldn't mind seeing those hazel eyes fixed on him with a feminine interest. There'd been a moment at the gas station yesterday, a brief flicker of connection.

Or was that wishful thinking on his part?

Not that it mattered, he thought as he pulled a can of soda from the cooler and popped the tab. Whatever spark might have been there seemed to have been extinguished when he busted her son. Still, this welcome party *was* in her honor. Not talking to her would be rude. He approached the table where the women were chatting. Mr. Ross stood a few feet off to the side, working the grill.

As Cole neared the group, he overheard Mrs. Ross

bragging about her son, Jarrett. "...so good with young people. He spends a few weeks every summer working at a horse-riding camp. It's a shame he couldn't be here today."

Kate's expression was a discordant cross between placating smile and deer-in-the-headlights stare. Cole experienced a twinge of sympathy. Were they already trying to fix her up with someone? Jarrett Ross was a good guy, but he was gone a lot on the rodeo circuit. Although Mrs. Ross might be eager for her son to settle into a steady relationship, as far as Cole knew, Jarrett was thoroughly enjoying the admiration of his female fans.

"It's also a shame Crystal couldn't be here," Kate interjected, surprising Cole by glancing his way. She was obviously desperate for a change of subject. "If her family had made it, your girls would have had more kids to play with."

"Luckily for me, the girls are pretty good at entertaining themselves. Mandy's happy as long as she has a soccer ball, and Alyssa..." He looked toward the tree where his daughter had been sitting. She was often content with quieter hobbies, like coloring or reading her favorite picture books. But she was no longer there.

Following his gaze, Joan Denby said, "She's with Luke. I watched them walk over that hill a few minutes ago."

"You're kidding." Last Cole had heard, his daughter was still ticked off at the teen. What had enticed her to wander off with him?

Joan nodded. "They headed in the general direction of the barn."

"Maybe I should round them up." Kate shot hastily to her feet.

Was she worried the two kids were into mischief? Cole didn't know Luke Sullivan. Had the kid's shoplifting been an aberration, or was he a habitual troublemaker?

"I'll go with you," Cole volunteered.

Kate bit her lip. Whether she wanted his company or not, it wasn't as though she could forbid him to check on his own child.

They fell into step with each other, making their way down the small green slope that curved behind the farmhouse. The barn was visible, the distance of a couple of football fields away, but he didn't see the kids yet. They might have been inside or around the corner, where the overhang provided shade. Kate was quiet as they walked, her gait stiff. He attempted to defuse the situation with humor.

"Could be worse," he deadpanned. "You could be stuck at the table, sitting through countless pictures of Jarrett Ross's rodeo buckles on Mrs. Ross's phone."

"Did I look as trapped as I felt?"

"So much that I was questioning whether I'd need my hostage negotiation training to rescue you."

Her lips curved in an impish grin. "Think Mrs. Ross would have let me go in exchange for a fully fueled helicopter and a briefcase of unmarked bills? Not that she was the only guilty party. Before she started regaling me with Jarrett's many fine qualities, Gram—*Oh.*" She sucked in a breath as her foot slid sideways, catching a root that jutted out from the hillside.

Cole reached for her automatically, his hands going to her waist so she wouldn't tumble. As soon as his fingers settled above her hips, a potent sense of awareness jolted through him. The only thing separating her skin from his was the soft thin cotton of her dress. It was an absurdly tantalizing thought, given the hands-on nature of his job. From shaking hands with voters to demonstrating first-aid techniques in community classes, his days were full of physical contact. Yet he couldn't recall the last time he'd been so deeply affected.

Kate, however, didn't seem to share his enjoyment of the moment. Her eyes were wide, as if she found his touch disconcerting. As soon as he noticed, he let go of her so fast she almost lost her balance again.

He winced. When had he become such a bumbling ass? "Sorry." This time he steadied her with a strictly platonic grip on her elbow.

"No reason to be," she said, her voice shaky. "You were, um, just trying to be helpful."

Exactly. Helpful. Not lustful.

Well, maybe a bit of both. "I didn't mean to startle you, grabbing you like that." The expression on her face had been damned near panicky.

"It's been a really long—" Her cheeks reddened. "I guess I shouldn't be tromping around the farm in wedge sandals. They're not exactly all-terrain. What was I saying? Before?"

The better question was, what had she been about to say now, before she'd interrupted herself to denounce her shoes?

She snapped her fingers. "Oh, I remember! Just that Jarrett Ross wasn't the only man Gram and her friends mentioned. There was also prolonged discussion of one of Crystal's cousins, an accountant named Greg

Tucker? Your mother can't imagine why someone who would be 'such a good provider' is still single."

"Possibly because Greg hates kids," Cole guessed. "Well, *hate* may be too strong a word. But not by much." From what Cole had seen when the Tuckers were together en masse, Greg barely tolerated his legion of nieces and nephews. He was a completely illogical match for a single mom.

"I definitely can't get involved with anyone who dislikes kids. Luke's challenging enough to people who *are* crazy about them." She pressed a hand to her forehead. "Lord, that sounded awful. I didn't mean... I know he didn't make a stellar first impression on you, but deep down he's a good boy."

"All kids make mistakes," he reassured her, remembering his own scalding embarrassment when he was called into the principal's office to discuss Alyssa's marker-on-the-bathroom-wall misadventure. "Even a cop's kids."

Kate's laugh was hollow. "That's exactly what Luke is."

He swung his gaze to her in surprise. "Your exhusband is a policeman?"

"Was," she corrected softly. "My late husband was a policeman."

He was too shocked to respond. Why hadn't his mother mentioned Kate was a widow? "I—"

"There they are." She gestured toward the left of the barn. The two kids sat with their heads close together as they looked down, too focused to notice the approaching adults. As Cole and Kate got closer, the breeze carried Alyssa's exclamations of delight.

"It's perfect!" she cried. "Except it needs wings."

Luke chuckled. "First you said you wanted a horse, then you said unicorn. Now a Pegasus? What's next, a whole herd?"

"No. I just want one winged unicorn. But she'd look better if she was glittery. Do you have any sparkly crayons?" she asked hopefully.

"Hell, no."

Cole's eyes narrowed at the kid's language, but Kate's fingers on his forearms stopped his intended reprimand. He glanced up, his annoyance fading in the wake of her beseeching expression.

Besides, his little girl was already taking the teenager to task. "You aren't supposed to say the *H* word. Unless you're at church and they're talking about the Bad Place."

"Sorry. I'll try not to say it again," Luke promised.

"That's okay. Sometimes my daddy says it, too."

Kate snickered, and Cole gave her a sheepish smile. "Busted," she said softly.

Luke's head shot up. "Mom?"

"Hey." She stepped away from Cole, putting an almost comical amount of distance between them.

Cole remembered the boy's hostility yesterday when he'd seen the two adults smiling at each other. How long had it been since Luke's father died? As someone who was still close to both of his parents, even as an adult, Cole couldn't imagine what that loss was like for the kid.

"We were just coming to get you guys for lunch," Kate said. "Who's hungry?"

"Me!" Alyssa shot up as though she was springloaded. Although Luke showed more restraint, his eyes gleamed at the mention of food.

Both kids hurried back toward the house.

"Be careful," Cole called after his daughter. Her flip-flops weren't any better suited for hiking across rolling pastureland than Kate's sandals were. He glanced down to check for swelling or a limp. "How's your foot? You didn't twist your ankle, did you?"

"I'm fine. Just a little embarrassed. I reacted badly when you tried to keep me from falling. I didn't mean to be ungrateful. But it's been so long since…"

A man had touched her? At all? Cole hadn't exactly swept her into his arms for a passionate embrace. "Did you lose him recently?" he asked in a murmur, as if his regular speaking voice would make the question disrespectful.

She shook her head. "Couple of years. But I've been so busy trying to keep Luke out of trouble that time gets distorted, if that makes any sense."

"It does. My ex-wife left when the girls were babies— she decided she wasn't cut out for small-town life *or* trying to take care of two infants. There are odd moments when our being a whole family feels like yesterday, but other times, it seems like a different existence, altogether. Like remembering a past life."

Kate nodded, looking relieved by his understanding. Neither of them spoke again until they were close enough to breathe in the spicy aroma of grilled sausages.

"Cole?"

Her soft voice brushed over his skin like a warm breeze. "Hmm?"

"If Gram starts another recitation of the town's Most Eligible Men, will you help me change the subject?

Please. I know her intentions are good—she worries about me being lonely—but I'm not ready to date."

After dozens of frustrating conversations with his mom about his own love life, or lack thereof, he empathized all too well. In fact... He stopped abruptly. "Maybe the two of us can help each other. I have a radical idea."

Chapter Four

Kate blinked at Cole's unexpected—and vaguely unsettling—declaration. "How radical are we talking?"

"I'll explain when we have more time." He flashed her the same endearingly boyish smile she'd glimpsed when his daughter had ratted him out for occasional use of the *H* word. "For now, do you trust me enough to follow my lead?"

He was using *trust* in a casual, conversational sense. Still, trust was a special bond, earned over time. An intimate connection. Errant longing rippled through her.

What is wrong with me today? Her emotional responses were all over the map. From the way she'd nearly bolted when he'd touched her earlier to—

"Katie? Everything all right?" Joan called with a frown. Everyone was seated, and it was obvious they were waiting on the two stragglers.

"Sorry, Gram. We'll be right there." Giving Cole a barely perceptible nod to signal that she'd take her cues from him—and hoping she wouldn't regret it—she strode toward the table.

"Now that we're all here," Joan said, "we can bless the food. Harvey, would you do the honors?"

The kids already had plates piled high. Once grace

was finished, they dug in as the adults served themselves.

Mrs. Trent smiled in Kate's direction. "Alyssa tells me your son is quite the artist."

Alyssa nodded happily. "They don't have horses here, but he knows how to draw one real good."

"Do you like horses?" Mrs. Ross asked Luke. She wasn't deterred by his noncommittal shrug. "Maybe you and your mom can come over sometime and go riding at our ranch. Then you can meet my daughter Vicki, who's home from college for the summer, and of course, Jarrett." This last was aimed at Kate.

Kate grimaced. Couldn't she at least have a moment to savor her grandmother's award-winning potato salad before the matchmaking brigade started in on her again? Some things were sacred.

Gram must have seen her reaction because she was quick to offer an alternative to Jarrett Ross. "You know who else has a nice stable of horses?"

Kate bit the inside of her cheek, desperately hoping that wasn't some kind of euphemism.

"Brody Davenport. He—"

"Ah, but Brody's so busy these days," Cole interrupted. "With Jasmine Tucker."

"Crystal's younger sister?" Kate asked.

"That's right. I forgot Jasmine moved back to town," Gram said, looking disgruntled.

"She was in New York for a while," Mrs. Ross said. "Modeling. Doesn't that sound glamorous? But she's back now and owns the most fashionable boutique in Cupid's Bow. Well…technically the only boutique."

"I should take you by there this week," Gram told Kate. "I'm going to town Tuesday afternoon for a festival meeting. You can come with me, maybe get involved with one of the committees. It's a great way to meet folks."

"Actually," Cole said, "Kate and the kids and I are going to the pool Tuesday afternoon."

"We are?" The words came from Luke but echoed Kate's surprised thoughts.

Cole nodded. "Since I couldn't take the girls swimming yesterday, I already texted Deputy Thomas about my taking off Tuesday afternoon. And when Kate asked if the community pool was as impressive as she remembered, I invited her and Luke to join us."

For a lawman, he was a surprisingly comfortable liar. They'd never discussed the pool. What if she had a terrible phobia of water or something? But the community pool *was* a huge recreational attraction. Decades ago, a family with more oil money than they knew what to do with had donated the funds to build the pool. It was far bigger than any of the public pools in neighboring towns and included a toddler play area, a spiral slide and two diving boards. Given that it was hot enough in Cupid's Bow to swim nearly half the year, the town council deemed the pool worth the extensive upkeep. Kate had been planning to take Luke soon, to help make up for the laser tag arenas and twenty-four screen movie theaters they'd left behind.

And now she was going on Tuesday, with a hot single dad whose merest touch made her nerve endings sizzle. *Maybe "I'm not ready to date" means something different in Cupid's Bow.* She knew Cole was sincere about the outing, or he wouldn't have mentioned it in front of their collective children. Was this where she was supposed to follow his lead?

"Thanks again for the invitation," she told Cole.

It wasn't until everyone finished and people began cleaning up that she had a chance to talk to him alone. Gram sent Kate to get a box of lawn games from the shed, and Cole followed along.

"I hope you didn't have pressing plans for Tuesday," he said sheepishly.

And if she had? She couldn't find it in herself to be annoyed, though. His unexpected fib had saved her from a meeting where she suspected she would have heard about many single male cousins, neighbors, sons and brothers.

"You said your grandmother worries about you being lonely," he continued as they neared the shed. "I'm in the same boat. Mom's been on my case about the girls needing a mother. While I don't disagree in theory, I'm not going to run out and propose to someone just to appease her. I already know most of the women in town, even dated a few after the divorce. But there was never any..."

She turned toward him expectantly, and their gazes collided. His eyes made her nervous; they saw too much. He must be hell on suspects with something to hide. Although, perhaps potential criminals being questioned weren't hung up on how blue his eyes were.

"...spark," Cole finished, his words an ironic counterpoint to the charged air between them.

Heat flooded her face, a mixture of physical awareness and embarrassment. Since Damon's death, no man had grabbed her interest. She hadn't kissed anyone, certainly hadn't thought about doing more with anyone. But when Cole had his hands on her after she'd stumbled, there'd been a definite *zing*. It felt like desire—or the way she remembered desire feeling, when it had still been part of her emotional spectrum. Experiencing it so unexpectedly had caused her to falter worse than the root she'd tripped over.

She attempted a casual, teasing tone. "No spark with anyone? Not even…Becca Johnston?"

He scrubbed a hand over his face. "Only been here a day, and you've already heard about her, huh? See, this is why I've been reduced to shamelessly using you as a human shield."

"I'm not comfortable pretending to date you, if that's what you're suggesting." She opened the door and stepped inside the shed, pausing as she waited for her eyes to adjust to the dim light. "I won't lie to Gram, and it would be extremely confusing for Luke."

"No, I would never feign a relationship, either. But I thought that if the two of us spend a little time together, maybe our families will take that as a sign of progress, be encouraged enough to get off our backs."

So he didn't want to pretend a romance, necessarily. Romance and Cole in the same thought left her momentarily dizzy, although maybe she was just reacting to his nearness. It was close quarters in here. She shook it off, trying to focus.

If the two of them spent a little time in the company of the opposite gender—namely, with each other— would their meddling loved ones relent? Starting a new life here in Cupid's Bow would be easier if she weren't worried about Gram constantly ambushing her with men. Plus, Alyssa Trent seemed to be a good influence on Luke, candy bar incident notwithstanding. The Pegasus he'd drawn might be only his humoring a five-year-old, but it was still the first illustration he'd done in months.

Maybe spending a little time with Cole and his girls would benefit them all. She and the sheriff were on the same page as far as intentions—this wasn't dating. It was a mutually advantageous arrangement.

"I'm in," she agreed. "But next time you announce our plans to a group, you should check with me first."

"Done. You just let me know what you need. We can spend time out and about, introducing you and Luke to as many townspeople as possible, or we can stick to activities like going to the movies, where we don't have to interact much at all but will still be seen together. You may not know it, but the Cupid's Bow Cineplex now shows up to three different movies at the same time."

"Wow. Three whole movies, huh?" Her tone was light, but inside, she experienced a flutter of anticipation at the idea of sitting in the dark next to Sheriff Trent, their thighs pressed together in adjoining seats.

You don't have to sit next to him, she reminded herself. They had children to behave as de facto chaperones. Although she and Luke had never really talked about her dating again—there'd never been a need— she doubted he would be excited about her cozying up to the town sheriff. Best to keep this platonic and businesslike.

And the sooner she got out of the small shed where she was close enough to brush against him with the slightest motion, breathing in the combination of his aftershave and sun-warmed skin, the easier it would be to remember that.

TUESDAY MORNING, Kate worked in the garden along-side Gram while Luke pulled some weeds that were crowding the front steps of the house. Kate was proud of him—though he hadn't exactly volunteered to help outside instead of playing video games, he hadn't pro-tested when she enlisted him, either. The pool was going to feel heavenly after working out in the sun.

Gram adjusted her straw hat for a better look at her wristwatch. "We should go in soon if we want enough time to eat lunch and clean up. I've got that festival meeting today, and you've got your big date."

"It's *not*—" Oops. She probably shouldn't sound so defensive if she and Cole were going to make his plan work. Though she wouldn't lie to make it sound as if they were swept up in the romance of the century, she could at least give the impression she was open to possibilities. "I mean, we'll have the kids with us. It's hardly a candlelit dinner."

"And would you say yes if he asked you out for one of those?" Gram pressed.

No way. The thought of staring across a table into Cole's blue eyes made her palms sweat and her stom-ach knot. "I... He's an attractive man." Too damned attractive. "And charming." If a woman didn't have an aversion to dating a law officer. "But I'm just dipping my toes back in the water. I'm not ready to think about cannonballing into the deep end."

"All right." Gram studied the tomato plants, choos-ing a few that were ready to be picked before adding slyly, "But am I forgiven for not telling you he'd be at the cookout?"

"Just this once. No sneak attacks with other men."

"Well, of course not." Gram looked baffled. "Why

would I try to introduce you to anyone else when you and Sheriff Trent are getting to know each other?"

Cole's assessment of the situation had been spot on—without the protection of a few outings with him, Kate might find herself under siege. And once they stopped those outings to make sure none of their children misread the situation? Gram could invite whomever she wanted to the farm, whenever she wanted.

"I'm going to head inside," Kate said. "The heat and the empty stomach are starting to make me queasy." As was the prospect of a dozen gentleman callers, invited for Sunday dinner or to repair the barbwire fence or to check out an imagined sound Gram thought her car engine was making. Frankly, Kate was feeling a little nervous about the message she'd left this morning for the piano tuner. Was *he* single?

She went into the house and showered off the gardening grime, then started preparing lunch. When the phone in the kitchen rang, she reached for it, wondering if it was the piano tuner returning her call. "Hello?"

The last voice she'd expected to hear was her father's.

"Katherine?" He sounded similarly puzzled. "Is that you?"

"Yeah." It was funny—now that Kate was an adult, Gram still called her by the childhood nickname Katie; meanwhile, her father had always used her full name, even when she was a toddler. He'd been young when he became a dad, a college TA who hadn't shirked his responsibility when a former girlfriend left their baby on his doorstep, but he'd always seemed older than his age, treating Kate with formality. There had been hugs and bedtime stories, usually about indigenous peoples, but she couldn't recall him ever tickling her the way she'd seen Cole Trent do with his girls at the cookout. "Is everything okay?" she asked, startled to hear from her dad out of the blue.

"Right as rain. I call one Sunday each month, to check on Mother."

"It's Tuesday."

"Ah. Time gets away from me some between semesters. Now that I've got you on the phone, I can check on you, as well," he said, sounding pleased with his own efficiency. "How long will you be visiting Cupid's Bow?"

"Luke and I moved here, remember?"

"Yes, of course. And are the two of you all settled in?"

"Getting there. Gram threw a welcome party for us, and we made some friends. We're going to meet them at the community pool after lunch."

"Good, good. Your grandmother always did know what was best for you."

Once Gram had taken the phone from her and Kate resumed dicing up boiled eggs for salads, her thoughts returned to Cole Trent. He'd commented that people kept telling him the twins needed a mother, but he obviously adored his girls. She couldn't envision him dumping his children on Mr. and Mrs. Trent, relieved to wash his hands of parenting for a few months. Plenty of fathers out there weren't trying nearly as hard as he seemed to be. She was confident Cole could raise his daughters successfully as a single parent.

It was important she believe that. Because maybe, if *he* could do it, she could, too.

THE PARKING LOT at the pool was pretty packed for a weekday afternoon. Kate climbed out of her car, glad she and Cole had agreed to meet there. His picking her up would have made no sense geography-wise, since Gram's farm was in the opposite direction, and it would have made the outing feel too much like a date. Tugging the hem of the V-necked bathing suit cover that had bunched up while she drove, she turned to Luke.

"You're okay with joining Cole and his daughters for a couple of hours, right? He was just being neighborly when he invited us. That's the kind of town Cupid's Bow is."

Her son stared at her, one eyebrow raised. "It's fine. But you've asked me three times. Why are you being weird?"

Excellent question.

"Sorry." She reached into the back seat for the massive beach bag that held their towels, Luke's goggles and enough sunscreen to protect a small village.

"Luke!" The high-pitched greeting preceded the slap of footsteps on the pavement.

Kate glanced up to see Alyssa barreling toward them in the same flip-flops she'd worn Sunday. Cole and Mandy followed at a more leisurely pace. Alyssa stopped in front of Luke, holding up her hand for a high five. Kate worried that, at some point, her jaded thirteen-year-old might decide it was uncool to have a five-year-old girl as a friend. Thankfully, now was not that point.

He smacked his palm against Alyssa's. "Ready to go swimming?"

"Yep. Daddy has my goggles and my floaties and

I'm wearing my favorite bathing suit." It was a rainbow-colored bikini top with a matching swim skirt.

Her sister was in a sportier one-piece. Kate tried not to think about her own bathing suit. She and Luke had been swimming half a dozen times in the past year, and she'd never once considered the teal tankini immodest. Now, however, she couldn't stop obsessing over the sliver of abdomen that would be exposed once she removed her hooded cover-up. She was a woman who'd given birth; her midsection was no longer the taut skin of a twentysomething. But so what? She wouldn't exactly stand out at the pool.

Yet the idea of being in front of Cole in so little clothing was irrationally alarming. She couldn't even say whether her apprehension was because he wouldn't like what he saw…or because he might like it just fine.

There'd been a couple of times at Gram's farm when his gaze had locked with hers, and she'd felt tingly, as if parts of her that had been long numb were slowly buzzing back to life beneath his notice. It stung, like trying to stand on a foot that had fallen asleep. She wanted no part of the accompanying pins and needles.

So she didn't quite meet his eyes when she said, "Afternoon."

"Kate." His voice was warm and rich. "Good to see you, again."

As the five of them crossed the parking lot, he explained that he and the girls had season passes to the pool. They waited off to the side while Kate purchased admission for her and Luke. On the other side of the ticket hut came the sounds of splashing and laughter and a classic rock standard being played through speakers above the concession area.

No sooner were they through the turnstiles than Mandy kicked off her shoes. "High dive, Daddy?"

He chuckled. "Let's work our way up to that. And let's find some chairs so we can put all our stuff down."

"What about my floaties?" Alyssa asked, sounding anxious.

"They're here." Cole patted the side of his duffel bag. "But are you *sure* you don't want to try going in the water without them first? You were getting really good at swimming." To Kate, he explained, "We went with some friends to the river a few weeks ago. The current was stronger than she bargained for."

"She swallowed so much water she puked!" Mandy said. "It was gross. She—"

"That's enough, Amanda."

"But I didn't even get to tell how..." She wilted beneath the blistering force of her father's glare. "Okay, okay."

"Kate? Is that you?"

Kate turned to see Crystal Walsh. "Hey!" She hugged her friend. It was the only time she'd seen the brunette as an adult when she wasn't pregnant. "I take it everyone's feeling better?"

Crystal nodded. "It was just one of those twenty-four hour bugs, thank goodness. The weekend was pretty miserable, but we're all okay now. The kids were getting stir-crazy so I asked Mom to stay at the house with the little ones during naptime so I could run the older two to the pool." She gestured toward a group of kids shouting in the shallow end. "'Marco' belongs to me. One of the 'Polos,' too. I wasn't expecting to see...you."

The mischievous lilt in her tone and sparkle in her green eyes made it clear she wasn't necessarily surprised to run into Kate; after all, the two women had spent so much of their adolescent summers here Gram had teased them about growing gills. The surprise was that Kate was here with Cole.

Crystal peered past Kate, waggling her fingers in a small wave. "Afternoon, Sheriff."

"Nice to see you, Mrs. Walsh. We missed you on Sunday."

It wasn't until Kate turned to include Cole in the conversation that she realized he'd removed his T-shirt. He'd balled it up and was in the act of tossing it atop their other belongings. *Holy abs*. She'd noticed at the cookout that he had a well-muscled chest and forearms, but her imagination hadn't done him justice. Now that he was standing there, shirtless and tanned, she found herself relieved he already knew her friend. Because there was no way Kate could find her voice to make introductions. Her tongue was glued to the roof of her mouth. Her eyes felt frozen. She couldn't look away.

Blink, woman.

"Mom?" It took her son's voice to break through the trance. "Can we get in the water now?"

"That's probably a good idea," Cole said, as he checked to make sure Alyssa's water wings were secure. "In another ninety seconds, Mandy's going to start climbing me like a deranged chimpanzee." The little girl was already impatiently shifting her weight from leg to leg, her face screwed up in consternation.

"What's 'deranged'?" she asked.

Luke laughed. Although Kate couldn't hear his response as they headed toward the pool, Mandy's subsequent shriek of outrage carried. With the four of them out of earshot, Crystal slugged Kate in the arm, smirking her congratulations.

"Girl, you work fast! Two days ago you're asking for information about him, and now you're on a date? There are women in this town who've tried for years. Becca Johnston's gonna *hate* you," she said gleefully.

Oh, good. Because one of Kate's goals for her first week in Cupid's Bow was to antagonize the town's cross between Watermelon Queen and the Godfather. "It's not like…" She chewed the inside of her lip, trying to decide what to say. If she assured her friend that Becca Johnston was welcome to him, then she wasn't living up to her end of the bargain. Kate was supposed to be Cole's shield against soccer moms and predatory divorcees.

Finally, she shrugged. "He mentioned that he was taking his girls swimming. I'd wanted to bring Luke here to prove there was something he'd like about Cupid's Bow, and Cole was nice enough to invite us along."

Crystal's expression faded from impish to sympathetic. "Luke's not too excited about the move, huh? I've never lived anywhere but here and neither have my kids, but I imagine starting over must be tough." She reached out to squeeze Kate's hand. "I'm here if you ever need to talk. I actually called your Gram's house this morning to invite you to lunch this week, but there was no answer. Then one of the twins starting crying before I could leave a message."

"How about lunch this Saturday?" Kate asked. Luke would be busy with his version of community service, giving Kate a couple of hours to herself once she dropped him off at the hospital.

"Perfect. My husband will be home with the kids. If you want, I can check with my sisters and see if they're available? Reconnecting with old friends is bound to make the move easier."

"Sounds great, thanks. And there might be one other thing you can help me with," Kate said. "Could you mention to other moms you know that I'll be offering piano lessons soon? If anyone's looking for a teacher..."

"Will do." Her smile turned sly. "You know, it might help you drum up students if word gets out that you and the sheriff are an item. All the women in the area will be super curious about you."

"Oh, I don't think it's accurate to call us an 'item.' This is our first...date." The word was simultaneously awkward and exotic on her tongue, as if she were attempting to speak a foreign language.

"Yes, but it took you only two days to get this far! He didn't waste any time. And who can blame him? You look fantastic," she said, her reassurance easing the misgivings Kate had experienced since shrugging out of her bathing suit cover.

"So do you," Kate said.

"*Pfft*. What I look like is a woman who's had five kids." But she said it with the easy contentment of a woman who loved her life and was comfortable in her own skin. "Come to think of it, I should probably double-check that my kids aren't trying to drown each other. I'll call you about Saturday. Meanwhile, enjoy your..." Her words faded into nothingness as they both watched Cole hoist Mandy onto his shoulders. His biceps and chest flexed and rippled.

"Well." Crystal sighed. "Just enjoy."

Actually, Kate didn't *want* to spend the afternoon

enjoying her view. She and Cole had agreed it would be bad for their kids to get the idea that there was a real romance brewing. Staring adoringly at him would confuse the issue. If she talked long enough about the risks of sunburn, would he put his shirt on? Plenty of guys in the pool, including her son, wore swim shirts. Of course, if she hinted that she wanted Cole to wear a shirt, he might realize how much of a distraction she found his bare torso. That was a humiliating thought.

You are a mature woman. Get it together. She trudged into the water, annoyed with herself for acting as if she were the same teenage girl who used to hang out here with Crystal twenty years ago. *You'll be fine as long as you don't look directly at his arms.* Or shoulders. Or abs. Nothing below the neck. Except that still left his killer blue eyes.

Luke had been absorbed into the group game of Marco Polo. Encouraged to see him interacting with some kids in his approximate age range, she gave him his space, gravitating instead toward Cole and his girls. Cole was trying to convince Alyssa to give up her water-wings long enough to practice floating on her back.

"I'll be right there with you," he promised. "I won't let you sink."

"But…" Fear crowded her expression.

"Oh, stop being such a chicken!" Mandy scolded. "You've done it before."

"Amanda, why don't you sit out for a minute," Cole said, "and think about how *you'd* feel if someone taunted you for being afraid of something?"

Kate half expected the little spitfire to retort she wasn't scared of anything, but instead she paddled her way to the side of the pool. Cole turned to lift her onto the edge. At the top of his rib cage was a puckered circle, white against the rest of his sun-kissed skin, about the size of a half dollar. Kate sucked in her breath at the evidence of injury. Her pulse quickened. Had he been shot, too? Stabbed? Had—

"Kate, are you okay?" He came toward her, his usual stride hampered by the waist-deep water. "You're pale."

"You were hurt," she said, her voice raspy as unpleasant memories and emotions churned inside her. "On the job?"

To her surprise, he laughed. "Nothing like that. This scar dates back to childhood. Horrible toy box accident caused by my brother William." Understanding filled his eyes. "Was your husband... Hey, Luke? Can you come keep Alyssa company for a minute?"

Moments later, her son was cracking seahorse jokes with the little girl as Cole led Kate to some steps in the only shaded corner of the pool. The water was cooler here, and they had the illusion of privacy. Everyone else was frolicking in the sunlight.

"Why don't you sit down?" Cole suggested.

"I'm fine," she lied, feeling like a first-class moron. She'd nearly had an anxiety attack. And over what, a freaking *toy box injury*? She grated out a harsh laugh. "Thank God this is not a real date. Can you imagine what a date would be thinking about me right now?"

"That you were married to a man you loved deeply and that you're still understandably sensitive about his death. That is who you were thinking about, right? Your husband?"

She nodded, covering her face with her hands. "Damon. He was shot."

Cole sat on the step next to her, radiating compassion. Pity would have made her even more uncomfortable than she already was, but this felt different. He was just a solid, reassuring presence, ready to listen. Even though she hadn't planned to say more, words spilled out of her anyway.

"I was always so proud of his job," she said. "He took protecting and serving very seriously. Luke saw him as a hero. But ever since Damon died, I get jumpy around people in that line of work. I can't stop thinking about how dangerous the job can be. I know you're all carefully trained, but…"

"If it makes you feel any better, Cupid's Bow is pretty low-key. Most of the crimes I deal with are drunk trespassers cow-tipping or the occasional loon trying to spray-paint a proclamation of love on the town water tower."

Yeah, but who was to say those drunks weren't armed? And being sheriff was a complex, county position. Cupid's Bow was his home base, but his job took him into other communities. Still, she appreciated that Cole was trying to make her feel better.

She smiled weakly. "You forgot candy bar theft."

"Yeah, we're definitely cracking down on that. There's talk of putting together a task force," he teased.

She laughed, starting to feel like herself again. "The community pool is a weird place for emotional confessions. But you're…easy to talk to."

"It's not me, it's the badge. Most people are trained from a young age that they can trust law enforcement, depend on us in a crisis."

"I don't know about that. Besides, you aren't wearing your badge." She was suddenly reminded of how little either of them wore. The concrete step put them in close proximity; his bare arm rested ever so slightly against hers. Their legs were stretched out together, hers looking uncharacteristically delicate next to his darker skin and taut calves. If she tilted her head just a few inches to her left, it would be on his shoulder.

Her heartbeat accelerated again, but this time, it wasn't the irrational panic that had pounded through her when she saw his scar. Her body was reacting in a number of tiny ways, all of which felt confusing and wrong after discussing Damon's death.

She shot to her feet. "I'm keeping you from your girls."

"Kate, it's okay."

"I know Mandy's itching to try the high dive with you. Why don't you take her, and I'll keep working with Alyssa on her swimming?" she offered. "I was a pretty timid kid myself. Maybe I can get through to her."

At the moment, Kate felt a strong kinship with the little girl. Because if there was anything Kate understood with perfect clarity, it was the terror of suddenly finding yourself in over your head.

Chapter Five

In the end, Kate didn't think she could take the credit for drawing Alyssa out of her shell and helping her enjoy the water. Luke was a natural with the little girl, alternately goading her like a resolute personal trainer and making her giggle. After she'd had sufficient practice floating on her back, Luke coaxed her to jump in from the side of the pool. At first, he'd stayed in the water to catch her. As she gained confidence, the two of them began jumping in together. Alyssa, merrily oblivious to the physics of water displacement, seemed determined to eventually make the bigger splash.

She jumped into the air, tucked her knees against her chest and yelled, "Cannibal!"

Kate did a double take, then looked to her son for confirmation. "Did she say—"

"You just now noticed? It was so funny the first time I didn't correct her." Then he launched himself into the air. "Cannibal!"

If Kate hadn't noticed the mispronunciation sooner, it was because she'd been lost in melancholy what-ifs. Since she and Damon had both been only children, it had seemed natural for them to raise just one kid. Being a policeman was a noble calling, but it sure wasn't a fast track to riches. Ditto teaching at a public school. They'd thought that by having a single child, they'd be better able to afford luxuries like memorable family vacations. They'd talked about seeing Europe one day. Her eyes burned with unshed tears. There had been so many things they'd planned to do "someday."

Now, watching Luke with Alyssa, she realized her son might have made an excellent big brother. Though he'd never specifically voiced a wish for a younger sibling, had he subconsciously wanted one? Kate had spent a lot of time during the past year thinking about his need for a role model. Maybe it would be equally beneficial for keeping him out of trouble to *be* a role model.

He bobbed to the surface of the water. "Know what we haven't tried yet, Aly?"

"Aly?" the girl echoed.

"Yeah. Short for Alyssa," he explained. "Like how everyone calls Amanda 'Mandy.' Aly can be your nickname."

"Oh." Her eyes widened. "Miss Kate, I have a nickname!"

"Anyway," Luke said, not sharing her fascination with the topic, "we haven't done the slide yet. Wanna go?"

Actually, Kate thought the little girl was starting to look tuckered out from trying to keep up with a thirteen-year-old boy. "I have an idea," she countered, "why don't we go to the concession stand first and get some slushies? Then you can reapply sunscreen and hit the slide."

Once they'd agreed on that plan, Luke jogged down toward the deep end to see if Cole and Mandy wanted to join them for a snack break. Alyssa scowled as she watched him go.

"Daddy and Mandy are probably having a lot of fun," she said, wrapping a giant pink princess towel around herself.

"I thought you were having fun, too."

"Yeah. But…" She stared at the ground. "Mandy always calls me a chicken. Like when Daddy makes us go camping. I get scared of the bugs. And camping is dirty. And when we camp at the lake, we hafta fish, too. Do you *know* how gross fish guts are? It's like the high dive."

Kate tried to puzzle through that comparison. "The high dive is gross?"

Alyssa shrugged. "How would I know? I'm too scared to go up there. Maybe Mandy's right. I am a ch—"

"Aren't you in ballet?" Kate took her hand, leading her toward the winding line in front of the concession stand. "Your nana mentioned your recital last month."

Alyssa nodded happily. "I wish ballet class was in the summer, too. I like to dance."

"And your recital was in front of an audience, right?"

"On a real stage at the big kid high school! There were really bright lights and costumes."

"Have you ever heard the term *stage fright*?" Kate asked. When Alyssa looked at her blankly, Kate explained, "Plenty of people are terrified to perform in front of an audience. The idea of doing a play or dancing or singing in a choir makes them feel like they might throw up. You don't sound like you were scared."

"Why would I be? Dancing is *fun*. Not like mosquitos or getting water up my nose."

"Good points. But the fact that you can get up in front of people without being nervous makes you a very special kind of brave," Kate told her. "You are not a chicken. Besides, it's normal to be afraid of some things. No matter how tough a person acts, everyone has fears. Including your sister."

"What about grown-ups?" Alyssa asked. "Do you ever get scared?"

Oh, kid, if you only knew. "Lots of things frighten me."

"You think even my dad gets scared?"

Probably every time he crossed paths with the infamous Becca Johnston. "I'm sure he does. Ask him about it sometime. Just remember, even though you're afraid of some things, you have courage, too."

"Thank you, Miss Kate." She repositioned her towel so that it was more like a cape and twirled in a circle, whooping, "Make way for Aly the Brave!"

"Wow." COLE WAS genuinely impressed as he joined Kate in line. "What kind of magic did you work on my daughter, and can you teach me your mystical ways?"

When he'd left Alyssa, her lower lip had been trembling over the possibility of floundering in the water. Now, she was spinning and shouting declarations of bravery. Mandy had joined her in the grass off to the side of the concession stand, arms outstretched as they whirled in giggly circles. Cole felt dizzy just watching his blonde mini-tornadoes.

Kate smiled. "Alyssa and I had a chat about the

different ways to be brave. I think she's feeling better now."

"Thank you. Mandy and I chatted, too. About calling people chicken and the consequences she can expect next time it happens." After setting his daughter straight about teasing, he'd planned to follow her off the high dive a few times, then come back to check on Alyssa's progress. But he'd let Mandy cajole him into "just five more minutes." Repeatedly.

She'd been having so much fun, and it was good exercise. *Plus, you were avoiding Kate.* Truthfully, he wasn't sure Kate had wanted his company after telling him about Damon's shooting. On the rare occasions he got choked up over something, he preferred to be left alone.

That wasn't the only reason he'd given her space, though. After she'd confided in him, he'd had an overpowering urge to take her in his arms. It was a completely inappropriate impulse, and he'd stayed away until it passed.

He'd expected going through the motions of a date to be more cut and dry. Mastering a degree of detachment was necessary for anyone in law enforcement. On the few real dates he'd been on in recent years, he'd never responded so strongly to anyone—emotionally or physically.

Of course, very few of his dates had included being half naked, either. At the moment, Kate had her arms folded across her chest, and he deserved a freaking medal for not staring at her cleavage.

It took every ounce of his discipline to keep his gaze trained on her face. Did she know how mesmerizing her eyes were? They were kaleidoscopes of color, with flecks of gold that reminded him of history class and the brief Texas Gold Rush. It had never amounted to much, but looking into her eyes made him empathize with the miners who'd temporarily lost their heads, beguiled by temptation.

"Where's Luke?" she asked, rescuing him from his fanciful thoughts.

"Oh, he said he'd catch up." Cole pointed to where the boy stood a few yards away, talking to a girl with a towel around her shoulders. "Um…did he happen to mention any drug references to Alyssa? Maybe jokingly? One of the locals informed me that my daughter was yelling 'cannabis.'"

"What? No, he misheard," Kate assured him. "She was yelling 'cannibals.'"

He blinked, not sure how to process that.

"So Luke's talking to someone around his own age?" She craned her neck, doing a credible job of trying to peek without looking as if she were watching.

Cole nodded. "Apparently the girl's beach towel bears the logo of some 'sick' video game. That's good, right? Luke commented on it, and suddenly the conversation became boss battles and cheat codes and a bunch of acronyms I couldn't decipher. I thought that, since he's still in our line of sight, it would be okay to leave him there. Do you mind?"

"Not at all. I'm relieved. School in August will be a lot easier if he meets other kids first. She looks about his age. Know who she is?"

"Arnold Pemberton's daughter. He's a trucker, and his wife's a nurse at the county hospital. I'm pretty sure the girl's name is… Sarah?" He glanced over his shoulder, hoping it would jog his memory. She was leaning toward Luke, who was a head shorter than she was, and laughing delightedly at whatever he'd said. "I'm also pretty sure she's flirting with your son."

"You think?" Judging by Kate's startled expression, girls had not been a big part of Luke's life thus far.

"Well, you're a woman—you tell me. What are the signs when a girl likes a guy?"

"I, uh…" Twin spots of color bloomed in her cheeks. "Oh, hey, it's our turn to order!"

Huh. Cole couldn't help thinking that, in his experience, stammering and blushing were *also* signs of liking someone. Or had his perspective—and ego— become skewed after months of Becca Johnston and other local women pursuing him? Kate was difficult to read. She was still deeply affected by her husband's death and had said more than once that she wasn't interested in dating.

Yet, at times he could swear the magnetic draw he felt was mutual. *Or maybe her flustered response was because you embarrassed her by putting her on the spot.* Maybe.

Regardless, as he placed his order, he found himself grinning with a lot more enthusiasm than an orange slushie warranted.

STARING THROUGH THE windshield on Saturday morning, Luke was no more impressed with the scenery than he had been when they arrived a week ago. It was so *flat* here. And rural. Still, despite the uninspiring landscape, he had to admit the last few days hadn't been all bad.

His mom had taken him to the pool twice, and he and Sarah Pemberton had exchanged usernames.

They'd spent a couple of hours Thursday in PVP mode, then gone on a campaign yesterday before the lag time got too problematic. Gram did not have the fastest internet connection in the universe.

His mom seemed to have a decent week, too. After the piano tuner had come on Wednesday, she'd spent a lot of time practicing. He'd heard her in the room they were now calling the "music study" singing along with the piano notes. It wasn't until he'd listened to her that he realized how rarely she did that anymore. She used to sing all the time, sometimes just under her breath while she cooked, other times really belting out songs, especially in the car. Half the stuff she liked was from before he was born, and he mocked her about being old. Secretly, he liked some of it. Bon Jovi wasn't bad.

Right now, they were listening to one of his Mom's playlists, but she wasn't singing or humming. Even with the music, it was too quiet in the car. He felt like she wanted him to say something. Would it make her happy if he admitted Cupid's Bow didn't suck as much as he'd expected?

"Are you nervous about today?" she asked.

He shrugged. "I dunno." He hadn't thought about it much. Helping Mr. Jacobs entertain sick kids was his punishment for giving Aly that candy bar. Luke supposed he deserved it, but the situation was weird. Adults said all the time not to talk to strangers, now his mom was dropping him off to spend half the day with one.

"Cole... Sheriff Trent," she corrected, "assured me that Mr. Jacobs is a good guy who's done lots of things in the community. Sponsors youth sports, played Santa Claus one year at the Christmas tree lighting."

Luke snickered at that, remembering the man's tattoos. An inked Santa?

"Anyway, if you have questions about what he needs you to do, don't be afraid to ask him."

He rolled his eyes. "I'm not scared of him, Mom."

"Good. And you'll have your phone on you at all times. Call me or text me if—"

"I know how to use the phone, Mom."

Her sigh made him feel ashamed, but seriously, did she have to talk to him like he was Aly and Mandy's age?

"How much farther?" he asked.

"About ten minutes."

"Can I get online when we go back to the farm? Sarah said she might be around." Even though she was a grade behind him, it would be cool to know someone at the middle school. She also had a brother in the high school who played football for the Cupid's Bow Archers. Stupidest mascot ever.

"Whether you get to play depends on how you behave for Mr. Jacobs and what Gram's doing this afternoon. It is her TV, you know." She paused, slanting him a glance. "Sarah seems nice."

"Yeah. She's okay."

"Just okay?"

He squirmed in his seat. He knew what his mom was asking, but he doubted Sarah would look at him like *that*. For one thing, he was too short. And his hair was starting to look ridiculous, long enough to hang in his eyes. "Can I get a haircut soon?"

"Sure. We can look for a place in town tomorrow, or you can go with me on Monday to Turtle."

He'd heard Gram and his mom talk about how there

wasn't really a music store in Cupid's Bow. But elsewhere in the county, where they had an award-winning high school band, there was a decent-size store where Mom could get sheet music and a metronome and other stuff she wanted for teaching. He didn't know what dumbass had named the towns around here, but he couldn't imagine going to a football game between the Cupid's Bow Archers and the Fighting Turtles. Sheesh.

Hoping to discourage his mom from asking more about Sarah, he turned up the speaker volume. "Isn't this one of your favorites?" he asked.

She snorted. "Subtle, kid." But she stopped badgering him.

At the hospital, they followed signs to volunteer parking. Luke couldn't remember ever being in a hospital. He knew his mom had gone to one after his dad's shooting, but it had been too late by then to say goodbye.

His father hadn't survived the ambulance ride. Luke had asked his mom once if she thought Dad had been scared. She'd said he probably wasn't conscious for much of it; she tried to make it sound peaceful, like he'd simply drifted off, without pain or panic, and never awakened. But that image had terrified Luke. For months after his father's death, he'd been scared to sleep, irrationally afraid he might not wake up in the morning.

The trouble at school began when he started falling asleep in classes, then irritably swore at one of his teachers. He'd met Bobby in detention hall. Talking to Sarah was a little like talking to Bobby because neither of them asked about his father. Bobby hadn't cared, and Sarah didn't know. Maybe Luke could make new friends here who didn't treat him like he was freaking delicate, didn't make him feel weak.

For the first time, he thought this move might work out okay. Even if the school mascots were ragingly lame.

He and his mom took an elevator from the parking garage to a main lobby, then followed a mazelike series of corridors to the pediatric ward. He found the murals of bright blue birdies and pastel pink bunnies a little insulting. No matter what you drew on the walls, it didn't change the fact that people were sick.

He started to worry that Mr. Jacobs might be going for some kind of cartoony image, too. What if he dressed like a clown to cheer kids up, or wore a top hat and glittery cape for his magic show? Worse, would he expect Luke to wear some silly costume? But Mr. Jacobs, who stood chatting with a nurse in the hallway, was dressed pretty much the same way he had been last time Luke saw him—black shirt, black jeans, boots. He looked like a man you'd see smashing a beer bottle over someone's head in a bar brawl; instead he was accepting a lollipop from a woman in Sesame Street scrubs.

Mr. Jacobs walked toward them with a grin. "Well, if it isn't my assistant for the day, Sticky Fingers."

Luke felt a blush climb his face, but at least the man didn't sound angry.

"Nice to see you again, Mrs. Sullivan. Are you still comfortable leaving Luke here with us, or do you want to stay for the shows? We have different performances for the younger kids and the older crowd. Splitting them up makes it easier to fit everyone in the room, too."

His mom hesitated as she considered the offer, and

Luke worried she might decide to stick around. With school being out for the summer, he saw her all day long, every day. He needed breathing room.

Luckily, she shook her head. "Thanks, but I have plans to meet a couple of friends for lunch. I'll be back at two. Luke knows how to reach me if you need me sooner. Be good, okay?" She reached out and ruffled his hair.

That settled it, he was *definitely* getting a haircut.

"Thank you for giving him this opportunity, Mr. Jacobs," she said. "It might be good for him."

"Both of you call me Rick, please. I have to admit, as far as assistants, I'm partial to Nurse Amy, the cutie who's helped me before. But she has more important duties. Maybe if this works out, Luke can come back next month, too."

Give up another Saturday when he hadn't even done anything wrong? Then again, at least the hospital was air-conditioned. Luke had decided while doing chores this week that it must be a thousand degrees at the farm. His mom gave him a quick hug goodbye, and Luke couldn't help grimacing at the display of affection.

"The thing about mothers," Rick said as she walked away, "is that they may cramp our style, but they love us more than anyone else ever will. I left home at seventeen, thinking I was too badass to need my mama, but I cried like a little bitty baby when she died two years later. Appreciate yours while you have her."

The thought that anything could ever happen to her caused an icy hand to clutch Luke's heart. He couldn't lose another parent. "Yes, sir."

"Come on, my stuff's in the big room at the end of

the hall and I need help setting up. I might even have time to teach you a couple of card tricks before we get started. At the very least," he drawled, "I can teach you enough sleight of hand that you'll be too suave to get caught boosting candy bars."

"That is never going to happen again," Luke said. "The stealing, I mean."

"Good. Maybe there's hope for you yet, Sticky Fingers."

"I SHOULD NEVER have let her join us for lunch." Crystal leaned across the table, complaining good-naturedly to Kate. "My little sister's life is so exciting that the rest of us seem dull in comparison."

Looking at Jasmine Tucker, known to friends and family as Jazz, Kate had no trouble believing the woman had been a model. All the Tucker girls were pretty, but Jazz was downright arresting. Her auburn hair was cut in an asymmetrical bob, highlighting elegant cheekbones and bright green eyes.

Jazz laughed dismissively. "Dull? With five kids? Please. They're always doing something to keep you on your toes."

"True," Crystal agreed. "How I'd love to get through the rest of the summer without a single trip to the ER."

"Besides," Jazz added, "life in New York wasn't nearly as glamorous as it sounds. There was a lot of getting up at four a.m. and waiting around. And rejection. And living in cramped quarters with roommates so we could afford rent. I'm happy to be home." She reached for the last piece of corn bread in the basket at the center of the table. "And, damn, I missed the food."

"Food's not the only thing you like about being back

in Cupid's Bow," Crystal said knowingly. "And I don't think reuniting with your sisters is why you're always grinning these days, either." Their other sister, Susan, worked for the county school district; Crystal had told Kate the two women should discuss teaching jobs, but Susan hadn't been able to join them today.

Kate couldn't help smiling at Jazz's obvious bliss. "I hear you and Brody Davenport are pretty much inseparable."

"It's bizarre because, on the surface, we have nothing in common." Jazz stirred her straw around in her sweet tea. "I'm obsessed with fashion and getting the boutique off its feet, and he's busy with his family's ranch. We have totally different interests and temperaments, but…" Considering how her eyes glowed when she talked about him, finishing her sentence wasn't necessary. "You know, I asked him out once, when we were in high school, and he shot me down."

"Which he has spent plenty of time trying to make up to you since," Crystal said.

Jazz smile was pure satisfaction. "Oh, yes he has. What about you, Kate? I hear you're seeing someone new. A certain local sheriff?"

Actually, she hadn't seen him since their afternoon at the pool, although they'd spoken on the phone. He'd called about piano lessons. Alyssa was hinting that she was interested, but Cole wasn't sure whether the sudden desire stemmed from an earnest appreciation for music or growing affection for Kate.

"You made quite an impression," he'd said. "She'll be heartbroken if you and Luke don't come to the girls' birthday party."

"I'll put it on our calendar," Kate had promised.

That had earned a chuckle and the explanation that he still hadn't figured out when or where the party would be, although their birthday was rapidly approaching.

"Ladies," Crystal sat back in her chair, beaming. "We have done very well for ourselves! Me, happily married to the guy I've loved since high school, Jazz practically living at the ranch with her hot cowboy, and now Kate is with dreamy Sheriff Trent!"

Kate was amused by her friend's enthusiasm, but quick to add, "We've only been on one date." The unfamiliar word was getting easier to say. "That's not exactly in the same league as—"

"Well, hey there, Crystal." A strawberry blonde who towered at near-Amazonian height stopped by their table. She nodded to each woman in turn. "Jasmine. And… I don't believe we've met?" She extended a hand to Kate, her nails painted the same frosted pink as her lipstick. "Becca Johnston."

Gulp. Kate shook her hand. "Kate Sullivan. Just moved to town. My son and I live with my grandmother out by Whippoorwill Creek."

"Would that be Joan Denby? Lovely woman. She's on my committee for the Watermelon Festival. I wish she'd brought you to the meeting this week. I can always use an extra pair of hands."

It was difficult to tell from her toothy smile whether this was an overture of friendship or an obscure threat to chop off Kate's hands.

"Kate's been pretty busy," Crystal said loyally. "Unpacking, getting reacquainted with the town, preparing to offer piano lessons."

"Are you? My Marc-Paul has a natural aptitude for music," Becca said. "Do you have a card?"

"Uh…no." Maybe she should put that on her to-do list. "Like Crystal said, I'm still in the early preparation stages." Becca didn't need to know that Cole was bringing Alyssa over Monday evening for a trial lesson.

"Best of luck," Becca told her. "I'll just have to keep tabs on Joan so I know when you're ready to take students. I have to dash, but it was nice to see you ladies. Crystal, you'll be at the parade meeting tomorrow?"

"With bells on."

No one at the table said anything as Becca exited the restaurant, catching up to the rest of her party.

"Is it just me," Jazz finally said, "or when she said she'd 'keep tabs on Joan', did anyone else picture her hiding out in the bushes, watching the house through pink binoculars?"

"She does seem a little…intense," Kate said. "But hospitable." After all, she'd encouraged Kate to get involved and had all but signed up her son for lessons. Kate needed students, and she needed word of mouth in the community. She suspected Becca Johnston could provide plenty of that.

"Not just intense, think the word you're looking for is *eerie*," Crystal said. "Downright eerie. We no sooner mentioned the sheriff and, *whoosh*, she materialized out of nowhere."

Jazz laughed. "She and her friends were seated in the other room and on their way out when she heard you mention Cole. You *were* being kind of loud."

"Comes from living in a house with five kids," Crystal said. "A person learns to speak up if she wants to be heard over the chaos."

The two sisters were still good-naturedly heckling each other when the waitress brought the bill. Crystal insisted on paying, to celebrate two of her favorite people being back in town.

"Do you have time to come by the boutique?" Jazz asked Kate as they rose from their seats. "I'd love for you to see it. And, you know, buy stuff."

Kate grinned. "Sounds fun, but by the time I got there, I'd only have a few minutes before I had to head back to the hospital to pick up Luke." She hoped his afternoon had gone well. She'd wanted to text him and ask for an update but after how prickly he'd become in the car, she'd received the message. No hovering.

It was difficult to know how much space to give a kid, especially one with a checkered past. It would be irresponsible parenting not to monitor him some, but she also had to give him room to be independent, to build trust.

There wasn't parking in front of the shops and restaurants lining Main Street. Instead, there were two lots at either end. The Tucker sisters had parked down by the pharmacy, while Kate's car was in the other direction, past the only bookstore in town.

She waved goodbye to them on the sidewalk. "Jazz, I swear I'll come by the store soon. And Crystal, I'll call you about getting the boys together." Her friend's oldest child was a girl, but she also had an eleven-year-old son. They'd talked about taking him and Luke bowling or horseback riding at Brody's ranch. Jazz had chimed in that Brody was an only child and, like Kate, he occasionally found it lonely. He'd bonded quickly with Jazz's nieces and nephews and claimed to love having kids around to liven up the ranch.

"As long," Jazz had qualified impishly, "as we can return them to their proper owners afterward."

After parting ways with her friends, Kate tried to stay under the shade of store awnings as she made her way down the equivalent of a few blocks. The town's movie theater dominated the center of the street, across from the bank. She was looking around, taking note of minor changes and marveling at how much had remained the same when she realized there was a man standing on the sidewalk in front of her. A uniformed man who'd yet to notice her because he was scowling at a window display.

"Cole?" It was the first time she'd seen him dressed in his khaki sheriff's uniform, and it made his profession that much more real. He was no longer just the doting father who'd kicked a soccer ball in Gram's front yard or the dad who'd given his daughters piggyback rides in the pool. This man oversaw everything from traffic violations to local manhunts to security at the county courthouse. He exuded power and authority.

"Hey." His lips curved in a smile so welcoming it sent a shiver dancing up her spine. When was the last time anyone had looked that happy to see her?

Well, Gram was always thrilled when Kate showed up, but there was a decidedly wolfish quality to Cole's grin that Gram didn't have.

"You're a sight for sore eyes," he told her.

"Thank you. And you look...very official." His badge glinted in the sun, and the dark green tie he wore was a classy touch. Aware that her physical perusal was lasting a beat too long to be casual, she turned to see what he'd been looking at with such exasperation.

They were in front of the toy store. On the other

side of the glass, rows and rows of dolls stared back at them, from baby dolls whose boxes were captioned with promises to "spit up, just like a real infant!" to fashion dolls whose separately sold wardrobes and accessories probably added up to one of Kate's car payments.

"Is it just me," Cole said out the side of his mouth, "or do their eyes follow you wherever you move?" He rocked from one side to the other, keeping a wary gaze on the dolls. "Why would a girl ever want one of those things?"

"Ah. Birthday shopping?" she guessed.

"More like preshopping investigation. I'm on my lunch break. I grabbed a sandwich at the deli and decided to stroll through town, do a little window-shopping for inspiration." He sighed. "Mandy's easy to buy for. I got her a pair of rainbow-striped shin guards, a fishing rod that's a miniature version of mine and the next two books in a series she likes about a crime-fighting panda. Alyssa...I don't know. At first, a doll seemed like a good idea, but I'm not sure if I could sleep with one of those things in my house."

Kate smirked. "I promised your daughter that even her big, strong dad was afraid of something. I just didn't realize it would be baby dolls. But I have to admit, they freaked me out a bit when I was a kid." Something about the plastic faces that were so human and inhuman at the same time. "How about a stuffed animal instead? More cuddly, less creepy."

"That's smart. I mean, she already has a bunch, but she seems to love them all. I can find her a cute teddy bear. And the sporting goods store had a pink fishing pole that—"

"You do know she hates fishing?" she interrupted, imagining the disappointed expression on Alyssa's face when she opened that gift.

"Alyssa? No, she doesn't. We fish every time we go camping, and—"

"Oh, boy." Apparently, the girl who'd had no trouble opening up to Kate hadn't confided her true feelings about either activity to her dad. Had he really not noticed her lack of enthusiasm? "Cole, I don't think she likes to camp, either."

"What?" He rocked back on his heels, his forehead puckering. "Are you sure you aren't taking some remark out of context? This is the same girl who cries cannibal instead of cannonball, so you have to take what she says with a grain of salt."

"This was pretty clear cut. I hate to break it to you, but she talked about how she doesn't like camping because it's dirty and there are bugs. And because you make her go fishing."

"*Make* her? But the girls… They've always been excited about our trips."

Both of them? Kate didn't think so. She recalled Alyssa's pinched expression when she'd commented that her dad and Mandy were probably having a lot of fun in the deep end. Without her.

Kate took a deep breath. "You and I haven't known each other long, and I don't want to overstep or sound like I'm criticizing…" Especially since her only child was currently working off his candy-bar debt to the business owner he'd robbed. What the hell did she know about perfect parenting?

Cole surprised her with a sunny smile. "Whatever it is, you don't have to worry about hurting my feelings. Years with my mother have given me a thick hide when it comes to surviving unsolicited advice. Besides—" he reached down to squeeze her hand "—I trust your opinion."

He did? She glanced down, watching the slide of his fingers across hers as he dropped his arm back to his side. For a moment, she couldn't recall what she'd intended to say.

"Goodness gracious." A feminine voice trilled from across the street. "We just keep running into each other today!"

Kate glanced over to see Becca Johnston and her two friends emerging from the flower shop. Becca marched across the street, not bothering to check for traffic. Granted, with Main Street being a mostly pedestrian area, there were rarely cars. But there was something about the commanding woman that suggested she could halt oncoming vehicles using only the power of her mind.

At Becca's approach, Cole stiffened. Without thinking, Kate reached for his hand, meaning to repay the brief gesture of encouragement he'd given her a moment ago. But Cole not only laced his fingers through hers, he used their shared grasp to tug her even closer, pulling her against him. He rubbed his thumb over Kate's surprisingly sensitive palm, and her breath caught. That shouldn't feel so good. Or so personal, like an activity unfit for a public street.

"Sheriff Trent." Becca's eyes narrowed as she stared at their joined hands, "I'm so glad to see you. The festival committee hopes to recruit you for a fun volunteer opportunity. We have an idea that will not only be an exciting addition to the last day of the festival, it will help raise money for an important cause."

"Thanks for thinking of me," Cole said, his cordial tone threaded with trepidation. Kate mentally added "festival committee" to his list of fears, right under "dolls who follow you with their glass eyes."

He cleared his throat. "But as I said last year, when I got asked to man the kissing booth, I really need to stay available for crowd control and security."

Kissing booth? Kate bit the inside of her cheek to keep from laughing. She could just imagine the long line for a shot at the sheriff's lips.

"Ugh." Becca wrinkled her nose. "Kissing booths are unsanitary. We will not be doing that on my watch. What I have in mind would only pull you out of the crowd for a few minutes on Saturday, then you could get right back to work."

Becca's friends had joined her on the sidewalk and were both bobbing their heads in supportive agreement. "Becca's thought of everything," one of them chirped.

Undoubtedly.

"You know how on the Saturday of the festival we've traditionally sold grilled hamburgers and hot dogs, with the proceeds going to the fireman's fund?" Becca asked. "I know how to drive that amount even higher."

Gram had mentioned that one of Cole's brothers was a firefighter. Whatever favor Becca planned to ask, she wasn't making it easy for him refuse.

"This year, I'm thinking…" She paused dramatically. "Bachelor auction! We'll call it Heroes and Hamburgers. While people are sitting down to lunch, we'll auction off dates—to be scheduled for a later time—with local heroes like firefighters and policemen. The committee brainstormed almost a dozen candidates. Deputy Thomas is single and your brother William. And of course there's *you*." She smiled expectantly.

"Oh, I, uh…" If Cole pulled Kate any closer, she would be inside his uniform with him. Lord, he smelled good. "There are different degrees of being single," he hedged.

Kate shifted, resting her head on his shoulder—both to lend credence to their implied relationship and because she simply couldn't resist the opportunity. Unlike when she'd felt unnerved by his closeness in Gram's shed, there was no risk here. Under the guise of his "human shield," she was free to indulge any reckless impulses she would otherwise suppress.

Becca's smile had become a tight mask. It looked so inflexible Kate was surprised the woman could still form words. "So you two *are* dating? Kate can bid on you. The more people who participate, the more money we raise."

Oh, yeah, Kate could bid—assuming the First Bank of Cupid's Bow offered bachelor auction loans. If not, she had a feeling she knew exactly who would win a date with Cole.

"Besides," Becca added in a silky tone, "even if some other woman does land you for an evening, I'm sure Kate understands that it's for a good cause. She and I were just talking in the Smoky Pig about how she could help with the festival."

Cole's gaze swung to meet hers. "You were?" His surprise was lined with betrayal, as if he'd caught her fraternizing with the enemy.

"It came up in a roundabout way," Kate admitted, feeling guilty that she hadn't warned him Becca was in the vicinity. She decided to make it up to him by rescuing him from this conversation. Straightening, she flashed a broad smile at the other woman. "Tell you what, give me a few days to warm him up to this auction idea, and we'll get back to you. Now, if you ladies will excuse us, Cole was just walking me to my car. I'm afraid I'm running late."

Cole seized the opportunity for escape. As the three women called their farewells, his long-legged stride took the sidewalk whole squares at a time. He held Kate's hand all the way down the street, not letting go until they'd rounded the corner into the public parking lot. Then he swept her into his arms for an exuberant hug.

"Well played!" Admiration danced in his blue eyes like sunlight on ocean waves. "Advice on Alyssa's birthday gift *and* you helped convince Becca I'm off the market? I could kiss you."

She inhaled sharply, but it didn't seem to put any air in her lungs. "It's, ah, probably best if you don't." She started to take a step backward, but there was a car in her way.

"Oh, I don't know." His voice dropped lower. "Becca's got spies everywhere."

"Cole, I…" Her voice was husky, unfamiliar. Though he was no longer touching her, he stood so damned close her thoughts were short-circuiting. Could she allow herself to kiss him in the name of convincing Becca he was taken? A flimsy excuse, at best, but so tempting. She swallowed. "I have to go."

"Can I call you later? We didn't finish our conversation."

The one where she'd been pointing out potential mistakes he was making as a parent? It was so flattering to know he valued her opinion. Exhilarating, even. To hell with the jittery butterflies in her stomach. Hadn't she recently given a lecture on bravery? Maybe it was time Kate reclaimed some of her own.

She lifted up on her toes, pressing a quick kiss against his lips. It was a peck, nothing more, but effervescent giddiness fizzed through her. She'd surprised herself—and she could tell from his sudden, absolute stillness that she'd shocked him.

"Just in case any of Becca's spies are watching," she murmured.

"Right."

"So… I'll be waiting for that call. You have Gram's number. Now, I really, really have to go. I'm not even sure it's mathematically possible to get to the hospital on time. Not while obeying the speed limit, anyway."

Cole's gaze captured hers, his grin wicked. "On the record, I would never condone a traffic violation. Off the record? If anyone has a shot at talking her way out of a ticket today, it's you."

She grinned in return, twirling her key ring around her fingers. As she climbed into her car, she thought it might be worth speeding if the result was Cole chasing after her. *Yeah, but what then, genius?* Everything she'd told him about needing to focus on Luke, about her hyperawareness of the dangers of a policeman's job, still held true.

Hypothetically, being chased might be fun. But in reality, she wasn't ready to be caught.

Chapter Six

It was like something out of a pod-person science fiction film. Except, Kate mused as she handed the salad dressing across the table to Gram, she was pretty fond of the alien who'd replaced her son. Ever since she'd picked him up at the hospital, Luke had been uncharacteristically animated. Rick Jacobs was getting a thank-you note in the near future, accompanied by a plate of brownies.

Luke had played video games before dinner, and Kate overheard him telling Sarah through his headset all about the kids he'd met today and about the motorcycle Rick was rebuilding and how the two of them were already brainstorming ways to improve on the entertainment for next month. After dinner, Luke eagerly helped load the dishwasher and waved Kate and Gram into the living room so he could perform a few magic tricks he'd learned.

Gram was impressed. She clapped her hands, then turned to Kate next to her on the couch. "Either your son is a natural illusionist, or my eyesight's going a lot faster than I thought."

Kate laughed. "No, he nailed it. Good job, kiddo.

Maybe the middle school here has an annual talent show."

"School talent shows? Lame, Mom." But he grinned as he said it.

The three of them spent a rather enjoyable evening together, watching a competitive reality show and exchanging comments on their favorite singers. The entertaining color commentary from Luke and Gram was almost enough to distract Kate from the phone that wasn't ringing. When Cole had mentioned calling, had he meant tonight or a more generic "later"? Maybe he was too busy. Or he'd forgotten.

During a commercial, Kate realized Gram was nodding off. Kate gently shook her awake. "How about we get you to bed? You'll be a lot more comfortable there."

"True." Gram gave her a sleepy smile. "Guess I can't stay up as late as you young people anymore. Goodnight, Katie." She blew Luke a kiss, then shuffled down the hallway.

Luke rose from the chair he'd been sprawled in, pulling the ever-present earbuds from the pocket of his shorts. "I'm going to watch some YouTube videos in bed, okay?"

"Only the channels and vloggers we've already agreed on," she reminded him.

"I know, Mom."

"I love you," she called after him.

He smiled over his shoulder. "I know that, too."

Alone in the room, she switched off the television and the lamp. There was a full moon tonight. So much light spilled through the windows that she had no trouble seeing where she was going. She went to her room and pulled on a soft purple nightshirt that fell to her knees, then padded barefoot to the kitchen, telling herself she was going for a glass of water. But she was peering into the freezer and weighing ice cream options when the phone rang, making her jump.

"H-hello?"

"Did I wake you?" Cole's tone was contrite.

"Not at all." A silly grin stretched across her face, and she closed the freezer door. "Luke and I just turned off the TV a few minutes ago."

"I meant to call earlier, but it turned out to be a pretty active Saturday night. What is it about a full moon that makes people more rambunctious? I just dropped off a drunken nineteen-year-old with his extremely angry parents, down the road from your Gram's place." He paused. "Any chance you want to talk in person?"

"Yes." Anticipation thudded in her veins. "But Gram's already turned in for the night. I'll meet you on the front porch."

"See you in a minute."

Should she change back into her clothes, or just throw on a robe? She wasn't wearing any makeup, but it was dark out, so she brushed that thought aside. She slid on her music note slippers and belted a black robe around her waist. Then she flipped her head over and brushed her hair, fluffing it into shiny waves that fell against her shoulders.

She was just pulling two cold beers left over from Gram's cookout from the fridge when a pair of headlights illuminated the front half of the house. She tossed a rawhide bone to Patch to keep the dog busy instead of whining at the front door to join them. Then she stepped outside, hoping Luke didn't emerge from his room to catch her flirting with a man in her pajamas.

Watching Cole unfold himself from the driver seat highlighted how tall he was. Tonight, he wore his hat with his uniform. He looked very official. And very masculine.

She waited for him on the top step, holding out one frosty beer. It was a nice counterpoint to the heat that lingered long after sundown. "You're off duty now, right?"

"Yes. And thank you."

Aside from a small wrought-iron table, there were only two pieces of furniture on the porch—the padded bench swing and Gram's rocker in the far corner, where she liked to sip her morning coffee and watch the sun rise. Kate wasn't ready yet to sit in the swing with him; the proximity might cause her to forget the things she'd meant to say. Instead, she took a moment to gather her thoughts, sipping her beer and studying the breathtaking sky. So many twinkling stars were crowded together that it seemed impossible to pick out individual constellations.

"Wow." She leaned her head against the railing, marveling at the sight. She'd have to bring Luke out here some evening. "Living in the city, I forgot how beautiful this was. We didn't have stars like this in Houston."

"Actually," Cole teased, "I think the stars are the same no matter where you are. It's where you are that gives you a different perspective."

That was true of a lot more than stars. If she were someone other than Officer Damon Sullivan's widow, she would feel completely different about standing here in the dark with the all too appealing sheriff. She might not be staring at the sky in an attempt to keep platonic distance between them. If she were Becca or one of the other women from town… A giggle escaped her.

"Something funny?" Cole asked.

"Sorry. I was thinking about Becca. She'd probably kill to be in my fuzzy slippers right now."

"I am very glad it's you here with me."

She was glad, too. She just couldn't bring herself to say it.

"So." He cleared his throat. "Before Becca accosted us today, we were discussing my daughter. There was more you wanted to say?"

"Obviously, I don't know you and your girls very well." It was weird to think she'd only met them a week ago. They already felt like an important part of her life in Cupid's Bow. "So maybe I'm off base, but sometimes outsiders have a clearer view of a situation. When we were at the pool, I got the impression Alyssa feels really left out. I think she hasn't mentioned how much she dislikes camping or fishing because she's trying hard to fit in with you and Mandy."

It had taken Kate a while to translate the girl's statement that fish guts were comparable to the high dive; they were things Cole and Mandy had in common that Alyssa did not.

"Damn," he said under his breath. "I know the girls have different interests, but I had no idea camping made her miserable. I wish she'd felt comfortable talking to me…or that I'd been more observant." He gave a bark of self-deprecating laughter. "I'm supposed to be skilled at catching clues and reading people! I wish I knew how to bond with her. Soccer and fishing are easy, but I don't think they have father-daughter ballet classes in town.

"Besides," he added, "the sight of me in a tutu? She'd be in therapy for years."

Kate laughed. "I don't think you have to go as far as a tutu. You just have to find a way to show her you value *her* interests, too. What have you decided for the girls' birthday party?"

"I haven't." Dropping his hat on the table, he raked his fingers through his hair. He sat in the swing and kicked his long legs out in front of him. "My mother keeps trying to take the whole thing over, and it's tempting to let her. She has a better understanding of the frilly feminine stuff than I do. But she also has an agenda. If I let her make the plans, the event could end up being me, the girls and a dozen single moms with their children."

Kate recalled having a similar suspicion about her grandmother's cookout. But there hadn't been a dozen men, only one very memorable man. Gram was a shrewd woman.

"I haven't hit on an idea that will wow both the girls," he continued, "although I guess we could just reserve a pavilion at the park and have another birthday celebration of cake, piñata and outdoor games. That's what we did last year." He grimaced. "And now I'm realizing all those games were right up Mandy's competitive, sports-driven alley. What if Alyssa didn't have any fun at her own party?"

"Oh, I'm sure she…" The kneejerk reassurance died on her lips. For all she knew, Alyssa hadn't enjoyed the party any more than she enjoyed the father-daughter camping trips. "There was cake and she got presents, right? She had to enjoy it some."

"Maybe. For two people who look exactly alike, they have nothing in common."

Nothing in common. It was the second time she'd heard that phrase today. "Oh! You gave me an idea." She joined him on the swing. "Your girls may have different personalities, but they can't be any more different from each other than, say, a small-town cowboy and a New York City fashion model."

He quirked an eyebrow. "Are you talking about Jasmine Tucker?"

"And her boyfriend Brody. Mandy likes outdoor stuff, right? And Alyssa begged Luke to draw her horses, so is it safe to assume she likes them?"

"As far as I know. But up until this afternoon, I thought she liked camping."

"Jazz excels at 'frilly' and 'feminine.' And she mentioned today that Brody likes having kids around. I wonder if they'd let us use his ranch one afternoon for a special birthday party? You could handle the invitations and all the food. Jazz and I, if she agrees, can make sure to add touches Alyssa will appreciate." Since Kate only had a son, she had to admit, it was fun coming up with ideas that were more girly. What if, in addition to standard face painting or temporary tattoos in the goody bags, she and Jazz organized small makeover stations?

Cole shifted, looking caught between gratitude and guilt. "It sounds like you'll be going to an awful lot of trouble on behalf of my girls. You sure you don't mind?"

"I'm a teacher, remember? I miss working with

kids." The sooner she got piano lessons organized, the better. Although, she had mixed feelings about signing up Marc-Paul Johnston as a student. She wondered if he was easier to manage than his mother. "Besides, your girls are sweet. Alyssa reminds me a tiny bit of myself at that age. We both come from households with single dads."

"Was yours clueless, too?"

"He was…withdrawn. Gram did a lot to compensate." She tilted her face toward him. "You are an excellent father, but we can all use a little help sometimes."

"My girls and I were lucky to meet you." He brushed her hair away from her face and tucked a strand behind her ear. Then he gave her a wry, lopsided smile. "But your generosity is making me feel really selfish."

"Selfish? You worked all night, then drove that kid home instead of calling his parents to come get him. Now that you're off duty, there are any number of ways you could be kicking back, but you're here brainstorming how to be a better dad."

"Maybe. I'm also the guy who sort of used his daughters as an excuse to spend more time with a beautiful woman."

"Oh." She didn't know what to say. The compliment sent little tremors of pleasure through her.

"And I've been thinking about kissing you all night."

Her breathing quickened. They both knew he didn't mean the kind of kiss she'd given him earlier. Was she prepared to offer more? Her sensual side had been dormant for over two years. Was she ready to open the floodgates? "I…don't want that."

"Liar," he said lightly. But he stood, giving her space. She was pretty sure that if his mouth had met hers, he would have overcome her objections in three seconds flat. She was relieved he hadn't tried. Ninety-nine percent relieved. One percent devastated.

"I've taken up enough of your time for one evening." He settled his hat on his head. "Thank you for the beer and the brilliant party suggestion. I'll call Brody Davenport first thing tomorrow and throw myself on his mercy. Will you talk to Jazz?"

"Absolutely."

She rose, deciding she might as well go in if he was leaving. The stars were still beautiful, and she supposed she could stay outside and enjoy the peace and quiet. But it was hot out here, making her feel restless and prickly. *You honestly believe it's the temperature making you uncomfortable and not thwarted desire?* No, but denial was her prerogative.

Cole opened the door for her. "Kate? I have five-year-old twins. If there's one thing I've learned, it's the importance of patience." He brushed the pad of his thumb over her lower lip, the delicate caress making her ache. "See you soon, sweetheart."

HARVEY TRENT RAISED his bushy eyebrows, shifting in his recliner to glance at Cole. "I understand pool parties and costume parties—there may even have been a toga party in my misspent youth—but what is a Runaway Ranch?"

Cole laughed; leave it to Alyssa to make her birthday sound as if it were being held at a home for troubled youth. "Not runaway. Runway."

Alyssa looked up from the sheets of construction paper she was folding in half for homemade invitations. Cole would be sending out evites, too, but why discourage her creativity? Some of the guests would appreciate the personal touch. "Runways are fancy stages, Paw-paw."

Both girls had been asleep by the time Cole got home last night. This morning, he'd called an extremely helpful Brody Davenport, then he'd told the girls about Kate's idea over brunch. They'd seemed excited, especially Alyssa, who hadn't stopped talking about it all day. He was glad they were at his parents' house for Sunday dinner so she had a fresh audience for her fervor.

The front door banged open, and Mandy barged into the house at her usual full-throttle speed. She went straight for the kitchen, either for something to drink or to plead with her grandmother for a predinner snack. Cole's brother William trailed her inside, holding a soccer ball and shaking his head.

"Tag, someone else is it," he said as he plopped down on the floor with Alyssa. The tallest of the Trent brothers, he looked like a giant next to her. "I should have stayed inside with you. This looks a lot less strenuous than trying to keep up with Mandy-pants."

"What's 'strenuous,' Uncle Will?"

"Short answer, your sister is a handful. What are you working on?"

"Birthday party invitations. Nana gave me paper and markers. But she didn't have any sparkly crayons."

"You think that's bad," Will said, his expression grave, "you should have grown up trying to share a pack of six crayons with two brothers. We didn't even have purple—we had to color something red, then go over it again in blue."

Alyssa's eyes were wide. "Is that true, Daddy?"

Cole laughed at his brother's version of the walking-to-school-uphill-both-ways speech. "No."

"Of course not," Harvey said, sounding affronted. "I made sure they had a roof over their heads, food on the table and adequate crayons."

Gayle poked her head around the corner. "I'm about to put the chocolate cake in the oven. Who wants to lick the beaters?"

Alyssa raced toward the kitchen. When properly motivated, she could move just as fast as her sister.

The three men turned their attention to the baseball game on television. Jace's favorite team was playing today, but the youngest Trent sibling wasn't here to see it. He'd bailed on dinner because of a "hot date." Cole assumed that meant it was a first date—at most, the second. With Jace's attention span, the flame often extinguished itself before a third.

During a commercial, Will told his brother, "Becca Johnston came to the station this week. Have you heard about her idea to raise money for the firemen's fund?"

"The bachelor auction?" Cole sighed. He really did need to give her an answer. And, considering the cause, he knew what his reply would be. He just wasn't ready to surrender yet. "Are you participating?"

"Sure. I'll probably drum up a lot of money in pity bids." Will had said more than once that the worst part of being dumped by his fiancée in a small town was that everyone knew. Hell, half the town had been invited to the wedding that hadn't taken place.

"Or," Cole corrected, "women with discerning taste will bid on a date with you because you have a heroic job, a way with kids and the Trent family good looks."

Harvey nodded. "Damn straight. It's in the genes."

"What about you? Going up on the auction block?" Will asked. At Cole's reluctant nod, his brother smirked. "Wonder how long Becca's been saving up, waiting for a chance to put her plan into action. You know, I hear she had a wealthy uncle in Turtle who recently passed. Maybe he left her an inheritance."

Cole chucked a sofa pillow at him. "You're making that up." *I hope.*

"Did you just throw part of my decor?" his mother demanded from the doorway.

William laughed. "Busted."

"Quit roughhousing and come to the table," Gayle said firmly.

While people passed their plates for servings of roasted chicken and three-bean salad, Gayle praised Will's decision to do the bachelor auction. "I think the event is a great idea," she said. "And while I think everyone understands it's just for charity, not necessarily a venue for romance, who knows what could happen? Maybe you'll meet a nice girl."

"Like Miss Kate," Alyssa said around a mouthful of chicken. "She's super nice."

"Miss Kate?" Will asked.

"Daddy's new friend," Mandy said. "She just moved here."

"She helped me swim better. And she says I'm brave."

"And she's coming to our party! It was *her* idea to go to a ranch. I get to have a cowgirl birthday!"

"And she's gonna teach me to play the piano!" The two girls spoke over the top of each other in their eagerness to extol Kate's virtues.

"She sounds really special." Will leaned back in his

chair, regarding his brother with surprise. "I can't believe this is the first I'm hearing about her."

Cole wasn't sure how to respond. He'd promised Kate not to lie outright about their relationship, not to embellish it to a point where his girls became confused. He'd already skirted the boundaries of honesty by cuddling with her in front of Becca Johnston and her festival-committee minions.

But holding Kate didn't feel like deception. It felt like heaven. He still wasn't sure how he'd managed to walk away from her last night without kissing her. She probably had no idea how alluring she'd looked, bathed in the moonlight, the breeze toying with her hair the way he'd wanted to do. Even her outfit of robe and fuzzy slippers, which had been more adorable than sexy, had generated lustful thoughts because she'd looked ready for bed. And thinking about bed in relation to Kate...

"Cole?" Will snapped his fingers. "Damn, you've got it bad, don't you?"

"Uncle Will! We aren't supposed to say the *D* word," Alyssa chided.

"Except when beavers build them," Mandy said.

Gayle berated her son for language at the table and Mandy asked her grandfather how animals like beavers and birds learned to build dams and nests in the first place, leaving Cole to his own thoughts. Which were dominated by Kate.

Maybe Will was right. *I do have it bad.* If he was this centered on Kate after only a week, how much worse would it be once he finally did kiss her? Because they were going to kiss eventually.

Weren't they? He understood that she needed to

take things slowly, but there was no mistaking the way she'd looked at him on her front porch. She wanted him. Whatever else she felt—and he imagined it was complicated—desire was somewhere in the mix. That gave him hope.

Knowing that he'd see her again tomorrow, for Alyssa's trial piano lesson was a kind of wonderful agony. He couldn't wait to be around her, appreciated every instance of getting to know her better, but it was difficult not to press for confirmation that she was attracted to him, too. *Do not rush her.*

No matter what his instincts urged him to do in the heat of the moment, he couldn't risk scaring her away. It had been so long since a woman had mattered to him like this, since he'd entertained thoughts of an actual relationship. This romance stuff was trickier than he remembered.

THANK GOD FOR triads and arpeggios. Losing herself in the familiar patterns of the keyboard and demonstrating major chords to Alyssa, Kate was almost able to forget that Cole was sitting in on the class, watching from the chair in the corner.

Okay, *forget* wasn't the right word. He had too much magnetism for that. But she'd stopped glancing in his direction every three seconds, so that was progress.

She'd agreed to his request to monitor the intro class grudgingly, which was unprofessional. With any other parent, she would have encouraged it. Quietly observing the lesson allowed a parent to not only get an idea of what they'd be paying for but to hear Kate's advice on hand positioning and practice times, which they could reinforce at home.

Cole had said they didn't even own a piano, although Alyssa toyed with the one at her grandmother's. He wanted to gauge his daughter's interest and see if the purchase of a midpriced electric keyboard was warranted. The feel wasn't precisely the same and not all keyboards had the touch sensitivity for volume control, but Alyssa could start learning notes and practicing rhythm.

At the moment, the girl's expression was filled with pride over locating middle C and playing it with the E and G.

"And that's a chord," Kate congratulated her. "Now let's try a scale."

When Cole and Alyssa had first arrived, the three of them chatted about music and the girl had expressed skepticism that all songs could possibly come from eight basic notes.

"But they can be put together in endless variations," Kate had said.

"What's 'variation'?"

"It's when you can do an activity one way," Cole had explained, "but there are a bunch of other creative ways to do it, too."

Kate's cheeks had warmed as her thoughts took a decidedly nonmusical direction. It had been a long time since she'd had to consider even basic...activity. Much less *variations*. Thank goodness Cole's attention had been on his daughter. If he'd glanced in Kate's direction, her face really would have gone up in flames. He'd gone on to illustrate his point with a painting example, reminding Alyssa that people could finger-paint or use a brush or, in the case of his repainting his daughters' room, even a roller.

"How was that, Miss Kate?"

Kate blinked, realizing her pupil had attempted a scale and she'd missed it because she'd been too busy thinking about Cole. And variations. "Um…you're off to a fantastic start, but we all get better with practice." Which begged the question, how rusty did a person's skills become after two years with no practice? The mind boggled.

Knock it off! She really needed to stop thinking about sex. Unfortunately, she doubted that would be possible until she got Cole out of the house. She'd had trouble sleeping after he left last night, tossing and turning. When she'd finally fallen into an exhausted slumber, it had been deep. This morning, she'd awakened with no memory of what she'd dreamed. But given the mental flashes she had whenever she looked at him, she could take an educated guess. The sooner he left, the sooner she would stop having those R-rated flashes.

Had half an hour passed yet? She discreetly checked her watch. *Eighteen minutes?* Hell. She was already feeling so high-strung that she feared what she might say or do in the next twelve.

She reached down for the bag next to the piano, wishing she'd left the sheet music she'd purchased in the car. That would have given her an excuse to exit the room and clear her head, or to send Cole away for a few minutes. "So now that you know what the eight basic notes are, I'll show you what they look like on paper. Once you learn to read music—"

"Hey, Mom!" Luke hollered a greeting as he entered the house. "Is Aly still here?"

Gram's voice was lower, but Kate could make out her reproachful words. "Well, *obviously* she is. Sheriff Trent's car is parked right out front. But I thought I told you we weren't going to interrupt their lesson?" It had been Gram's idea to take Luke out for ice cream earlier so Kate could concentrate on her work.

On my work, or on the sheriff? Because once regular lessons started, Kate didn't imagine Gram planned to vacate the house for all of them.

Despite Gram's valid reprimand, Kate was grateful for her son's interruption. Alyssa hopped off the piano bench and ran out to say hello.

"Maybe that's a good stopping point for today," Kate said, looking in Cole's general direction without actually meeting his eyes. "Let her practice chords and scales for a few days, see if her enthusiasm wanes."

"Okay." He stood. "But I wouldn't bet on it. She may be quieter than her sister, but she's equally stubborn. Family trait. When we get invested in something, we don't give up easily."

She recalled what he'd told her last time he'd been here, that he was a patient man. It was a seductive quality. Not only did Kate appreciate his control, it was heady that he considered her worth waiting for. Yet she couldn't in good conscience encourage him. Potentially wicked dreams aside, she couldn't say when, if ever, she might be ready to be more than his friend. Or his daughter's piano teacher.

Holding back a sigh, she exited the music room. The kids stood in the hall, where Alyssa was commenting on Luke's hair being "all different." He ran a hand self-consciously over the new cut. When the stylist had finished yesterday, Kate had been surprised at how much older he looked. He'd had the same shaggy mop, give or take a few inches, for years. *He's growing up.* And

Damon wouldn't be here to see it. To teach him how to drive or to give him advice on dating.

Gone were the days when Kate woke up unsure how she'd make it out of bed in the morning. She'd made it through the worst of grieving her husband. But it still caught her at odd moments. She could go for days on end without thinking about him, then *bam*. And the past week had been worse than usual.

She knew it was because of Cole. Was it the tangled emotional response of finding another man attractive that dredged so many memories of Damon to the surface, or was it the men's shared profession making her dwell on her days as a cop's wife? How could she ever be with a man who did the same job without being constantly reminded of Damon?

"Mom? You okay?" Luke peered at her with concern, then immediately raised his gaze to Cole, who stood behind her. The accusation in Luke's expression was blatant. Kate was on the verge of tears; clearly her son blamed Cole.

Mercifully, Alyssa steered the conversation to her birthday party, asking Luke to help with the face painting.

"What about birthday gifts?" Luke asked. "Know what you want?"

"A pony."

He laughed. "I don't think I'll be able to afford one of those, even if I help Gram weed the garden all week *and* offer to mow the front yard."

Cole reached out, cupping Kate's shoulder and she almost jumped. "Thank you, again, for suggesting the party venue. Both girls are *very* excited."

"You're welcome." Did it make her crazy that she

had simultaneous urges to pull away from him and lean into his touch? "Jazz thinks the whole thing sounds like fun. She's going to provide some funky accessories and stuff from the clearance rack of her boutique, and we're meeting at a big arts and craft store one county over to buy supplies for 'photo shoot' backdrops. I just hope Becca doesn't find out we're working on that instead of floats for the parade. Spending time on nonfestival projects this late in June may actually be against the town bylaws."

He grinned down at her. "Rebel. The good news is, if you get arrested, I happen to know where the keys to the jail are." He hesitated as if he wanted to say more, but then shook his head. "Alyssa, we should get home and make sure Mandy hasn't driven Nana crazy by now."

"Okay. See you this weekend, Luke."

"Bye, Aly." He high-fived her.

Kate expected the little girl to head toward the front of the house. Instead, she whirled around and threw herself against Kate's waist in a hug. "I love you, Miss Kate."

It was hardly the first time a kid had professed that sentiment. Heck, Kate herself had said the words to favorite teachers and piano instructors when she was a girl. *Don't read too much into it.* Kids were more open and spontaneous with their affections. Just because Alyssa had blurted an impulsive "I love you" didn't mean she was mentally auditioning Kate for the role of stepmother.

Trying not to blow the moment out of proportion, Kate responded the same way she did with kids at school. She squeezed the little girl back. "Love you, too."

Once the Trents had gone, Kate slumped on the couch, feeling drained. "Anyone want to watch a DVD?"

"I was about to take a bath," Gram said, "but you two can start without me."

Kate turned to her son. "You interested in a movie, or would you rather play online with Sarah?"

"Isn't that your friend from in town?" Gram asked. "She's pretty."

Luke jammed his hands into his pockets, staring intently at the ground. "I guess."

"You two saw Sarah while you were in town?"

Her son nodded, still addressing the floor. "She was in line with her brother at the ice cream parlor. He's old enough to drive."

It appeared the lively mood Luke had been in since volunteering with Rick had finally worn off. "Did the two of you argue or something?"

"No. Can I go to my room?"

"Sure." Kate was taken aback. He didn't want to watch TV *or* play video games?

She gave him a few minutes to himself, then went to investigate. It didn't matter so much that he told her what was wrong, just that he knew he *could* tell her. She knocked on the door, waiting for the muffled reply before she pushed it ajar. He was stretched across his bed on his stomach; he pulled out one earbud, his expression quizzical.

"Hey," she said. "I realize I've said this before and that I run the risk of crossing into lame territory, but you know you can talk to me right? It may be hard to believe that I was once a teenager, too, now that I'm so old—"

"Ancient," he said with the ghost of a smile.

"Right. But I might be able to identify more than you think." Back in Houston, he probably would have kicked her out of his room by now. But here, he didn't have Bobby and his cronies to confide in, so he might be desperate enough to take her up on her offer.

He sighed. "Sarah and her brother were getting ice cream on their way home from bowling in Turtle, and she said we should go bowling sometime."

"I see." No, she really didn't. How was the casual invitation reason to be upset? "And you're afraid you can't pick up the spare? Or that you'll look 'derpy' in the rented shoes?"

"Mom. Do *not* try to use my words." He sat up. "I like bowling, I guess. The problem is Sarah."

"You don't like Sarah?"

"I like talking to her online. When we're comparing sniper shots or divvying loot, knowing what to say is easy. It's not awkward or personal. But IRL..."

"Translation for the ancient lady, please."

"In real life. When I'm talking to her through the headset, it's fun. At the ice cream parlor, trying to talk to her made my stomach hurt. I didn't even want to eat my ice cream, but I was afraid to hurt Gram's feelings. I may throw up," he said.

So either her son had his first significant crush, or that stomach bug Crystal's family suffered was making its way through town.

"You've got a case of nerves. Like when Alyssa was worried about swimming without her water wings." Tactical error—Luke's glare made it clear he didn't appreciate being compared to a five-year-old girl. Kate held up her hands. "I'm not downplaying how you feel, I swear. In fact, I have the same problem. When I'm in a classroom, I know exactly what I'm supposed to be teaching or saying. But as you said, personal relationships are tough. There are one-on-one situations where I get completely tongue-tied."

Hopefully, he wouldn't ask her to elaborate. She didn't think her son really wanted to hear about the buzz of hormones she felt whenever Cole Trent got close. Or how the more time she spent with Cole, the more she second-guessed and triple-guessed what she wanted.

"My analogy about Alyssa was just to demonstrate that, most of the time, our fear of something is way worse than the actual consequences. She was terrified of swimming without the floaties, but as soon as she took them off, she had a blast. She didn't drown, she didn't get water up her nose. Swimming wasn't the hard part at all. The hard part was taking the risk."

"Yeah, that *sounds* good. I mean, I hear what you're saying. In theory, I'd love to be more badass. But it's hard to do IRL."

She empathized so much so that she overlooked the mild profanity. "You are one hundred percent right." *And I am one hundred percent hypocrite.* Was she really going to nudge her son to take risks when she, a grown woman, was too chicken to let a man kiss her on her grandmother's front porch?

"All right, lecture over," Kate said. "I'm going to pick out a movie, preferably one with cheesy dialogue and terrible CGI, and make popcorn. Join us if you decide you want some company. And Luke? Think about what I said. I won't force you to go bowling, but consider what you might be missing out on."

It was sound advice. Now she just had to figure out how to take it herself. How much was she willing to trade away to stay in her comfort zone?

Chapter Seven

Although Brody had assured Cole they could fit a lot of kids in the barn in the event of rain, Cole was glad the weather was cooperating for the birthday party. There was a soft breeze that kept the summer day from being too punishing, and the sky was dotted with puffy white clouds that looked more cartoon than real. But the best thing about today so far was that his daughters hadn't stopped smiling since they'd arrived.

Jazz and Kate had hung a banner over the cattle guard at the ranch's entrance that wished Amanda and Alyssa a happy sixth birthday. The slogan said Fun is Always in Fashion. Closer to the main house, the women had set up a red carpet where guests could get their pictures made. Or they could have their photo taken in the small corral where Brody stood with a shaggy pony. Kids who wanted to really get in the spirit of things could wear either a white cowboy hat and plastic badge or—for the more devilishly inclined—a skull and crossbones bandana and black hat. On one side of the barn were two booths for face painting and makeup application. Around the other side were games like horseshoes and plenty of folding chairs for parents and guardians to observe the frivolity.

From his current vantage point atop the sloping lawn, Cole could see Mandy winning a stick-pony race and watch Alyssa hamming it up in front of one of the photo stations. Giant posters were tacked on the side of the barn; his daughter posed in front of the Eiffel Tower in a beret, iridescent scarf and rhinestone-rimmed sunglasses.

Everything looked fantastic—especially the woman who had helped organize it all. When he'd gotten his first glimpse of Kate, he'd been speechless. He always thought of her as beautiful, but he was used to seeing her in casual settings. Jazz had applied just enough makeup to highlight her beauty and had done something to her hair, sweeping it to the side with a hint of curl, reminding him of vintage Hollywood.

"If you mock me," Kate had grumbled, "I won't be held responsible for my actions. Jazz said we had to look appropriately 'fashion forward.' I feel like an idiot. Grown women should not be wearing rompers."

He hadn't even noticed what she was wearing until then—and he wasn't entirely sure what *romper* meant but the bottom half of her outfit was shorts. The green color was gorgeous on her and although there was nothing provocative about the neckline or the silhouette of the outfit, when she turned away he'd noticed the skinny slit in the material that started at her neck and went all the way to her waist. It was such a slender gap, not truly revealing anything, but he found himself growing more obsessed with it as the day wore on. She was easily the sexiest woman on the ranch, no offense to the model who'd chipped in to make this day so much fun for his girls.

"Nice party, bro."

Cole turned to see his brothers approaching. Jace was balancing a paper plate on one hand and carrying a soda can in the other. After getting input from both his mom and Kate, Cole had decided the simplest way to handle food for this many people was to have it catered. A large table held aluminum trays of chopped beef and pulled pork. Buns were in plastic bags at the center of the table. There was a vat of coleslaw nearly as big as the birthday cake, and a wicker basket full of individually bagged chips. Earlier, he'd stared at a little girl for a full minute, trying to make sense of the design she'd had painted on her face before realizing it was smeared barbecue sauce.

Will wasn't carrying food, but he had two soft drinks. He handed one to Cole.

"How many people are *at* this shindig?" Jace asked. "Cupid's Bow isn't that big."

"We invited all the kids from Mandy's co-ed soccer team, the eight girls from Alyssa's ballet class and assorted other folks. Like their unreliable uncle who cancels family plans in favor of chasing women," Cole drawled.

"Dude." Jace gave him a look over the rims of his sunglasses. "Don't expect me to apologize for sowing my oats. It's not like the serious-commitment, settling-down thing worked out so well for the two of you, Dumped and Divorced."

Will smacked their younger brother on the back of the head; Cole jabbed him in the shoulder.

"And you bullies wonder why I duck out of family events," Jace grumbled. "Not that there was any chance of my missing this. I adore my nieces."

"They adore you, too," Cole admitted.

"Probably because they consider him a peer," Will said. "Maturity-wise."

"I would never flip the bird at a children's birthday party," Jace said. "But know that I am giving you the finger in spirit."

Will ignored this, addressing Cole instead. "We're headed to sit with Mom and Dad and eat some lunch. My plate's already at the table. Care to join us?"

Cole hesitated. He should probably eat some of the food he was paying for, and in a little while, he'd be too busy supervising present opening and the paintball war he still couldn't believe he was allowing. But he was reveling in watching his girls enjoy their big day. "In a few minutes. I like this view too much to give it up just yet."

"I'll *bet*." Jace elbowed him in the ribs.

Cole followed his gaze and saw Kate, bending forward slightly to apply adhesive gemstones to a little girl's cheek. "Hey!" He barely stopped himself from covering his brother's eyes.

"We don't get to ogle our brother's girlfriend," Will said. "Not even when she looks like that."

Girlfriend? That was one hell of a leap, especially given that Cole had never even kissed her. It bothered him that his brothers used the term so casually. What if one of the twins heard? They'd pestered him throughout the school year about their motherless state, drawing comparisons to their classmates' families, and he didn't want to fill their heads with false hope. "Don't call Kate that. We're not… Technically, we aren't dating."

"But everyone in town is talking about the two of you," Will said. "And at Mom and Dad's, you let me believe… If you invented this relationship to get Mom off your case, I may have to kill you. Because now that she thinks *you've* found a wonderful woman, she's started in on me."

Jace, however, was delighted by Cole's admission. "You mean she's single? Then it's high time for her to meet the best looking Trent brother."

"You're not seriously considering hitting on her?" Cole demanded.

"What? You just said there's nothing between you."

"That is not what I said. At all." There was definitely something between him and Kate. He just didn't know how to label it. "Besides, she's older than you."

"Fine by me." Jace waggled his eyebrows. "Older women know things."

An involuntary growl rumbled in Cole's throat. "What I meant was, she is a responsible adult. You are not." The idea of Jace getting involved with a single mother was laughable. "She already has one juvenile delinquent in her life. She doesn't need another." The words were flippant, not truly a criticism of Luke Sullivan.

Despite giving the impression that he was a troublemaker when they'd first met, the kid was proving to be a softie. He was patient and accommodating with the girls, especially Alyssa, and when Cole had stopped at the gas station the other day, Rick Jacobs had added his own favorable opinions.

"I don't have to stand here and take this abuse," Jace said. "I can go sit with Mom and Dad and let *them* abuse my life choices. I think Mom's favorite phrase since I quit college is 'woeful lack of direction.' It's been a few years. You'd think she would let it go."

Though he was registered as one of the town's volunteer firemen, his steady job was bartender. Their parents didn't think it was steady enough—not that Jace was overly perturbed by their disapproval. "I'll catch up with you guys later."

Will waited for a moment, then asked, "So what's the problem?"

"With our brother? I have many theories."

"Come on, what is this hogwash about you and Kate not dating? The last time I saw you, both your daughters were raving about her and you were staring into space with the dopiest expression possible. I believe *smitten* is the word. So what gives?"

"She's a widow," Cole said, hating the word. Aside from the obvious negative connotations of loss, it was an oversimplification. Kate saw herself as someone's widow, but she was so much more than that. "Her husband was a cop. She says being around anyone in that line of work makes her jumpy, that she can't stop thinking about the inherent dangers of the job."

Will sucked in a breath through his teeth. He knew firsthand that careers could create major problems in relationships. His ex-fiancée had cited his job with the fire department as a reason for backing out of their wedding. "That's…" He clapped Cole on the back. "Sorry, man."

The tone of sympathetic finality rankled. "Hey, I was just explaining why it would be premature to call her my girlfriend. I didn't say I was giving up on her. This isn't insurmountable."

"Are you planning to retire from law enforcement?"

"Don't be an idiot."

"And her husband is always going to have been a cop. No altering that. If she considers it a deal breaker—"

"Couples overcome obstacles," Cole snapped. Not that he and his ex-wife had. Neither had Will and Tasha. But some people did. He ground his teeth, missing the sense of peaceful contentment he'd been enjoying before his brothers interrupted. "Why are you here ruining *my* day? Go pop a kid's balloon or trip a little old lady or something."

Will looked sheepish. "You know I'm cynical for my own reasons. I didn't mean to aim it in your direction. But, Cole, if you already know something is likely to be a problem down the road, is it really worth going down that road? I've been through a breakup a hell of a lot more recently than you, so take it from me…"

As if she somehow felt she was being watched, Kate looked up suddenly. She glanced around and when she spotted Cole, a grin spread across her face. The sight of that smile hit him like moonshine, going straight to his head and sending a rush of heat through his body.

"Then again," Will amended as Cole waved to her, "*I* don't have a woman in my life smiling at me like that. Feel free to ignore everything I said."

"Already planning on it."

"THERE YOU GO! All done," Kate pronounced. She stepped back so the little girl in the soccer jersey could jump down from the chair. She'd asked for blue eyeliner and a blue flower on her cheek, made up of little gems, to match her team colors.

"Looks like another satisfied customer," Crystal said from behind her. Her five-year-old son was one of the invited guests, and she'd come to the party early to help Jazz and Kate set up. "Have you had a chance to eat yet? If not, I can take over here for a bit."

"Actually, according to your sister's schedule, all the kids are going to be herded to the tables for presents and cake in about three minutes. You know, I remember Jazz as being flighty when we were kids, but she grew up to be scary organized."

"She's having a lot of fun today," Crystal said. "As the baby of the family, she got bossed around by me and Susan a lot, and now you've put her in charge of something where she gets to tell a ton of people what to do. She's in heaven. Plus, she's handing out business cards and coupons for her boutique left and right."

"I'm glad. She deserves to get something out of today. Cole paid us for all the supplies, but I know she's donated some stuff from the store. He really appreciates it."

Crystal looked over to where Cole stood talking to his brother. Kate had met him when he first arrived; William Trent looked a lot like Cole, except taller and broader with the merest scruff of a beard dotting his jaw. "So how are things with you and the sheriff? I'm guessing pretty darn good since he can't take his eyes off you."

"That's an exaggeration. He's been busy with his family and the party guests." He'd had to break up a fight between two little boys earlier, and there'd been a minor first-aid crisis in the form of a bee sting.

It occurred to her that since she was so aware of everything Cole had been doing, maybe *she* was the one who couldn't take her eyes off *him*. He'd caught her looking more than once, and the glances he'd given her in return made her glad to be a woman.

"I'll say this," she told Crystal, "he does seem to appreciate the hair and makeup job your sister did."

"Yeah, there's a reason Susan and I both begged her to do our makeup at our respective weddings." She paused, giving Kate a sly smile. "Just a little something for you to keep in mind, in case things get serious."

"Crystal!" How had her friend made the leap from *one* date at the community pool to a hypothetical wedding? "I haven't even known the guy a month. And I'm not sure I'll ever remarry." She'd given her heart to Damon. It was difficult to imagine making that level of commitment a second time.

Crystal's teasing expression dissolved. "I'm sorry. Was that insensitive? It's just really nice to see you happy after everything you've been through. You haven't stopped smiling all day. But I was only joking around. I know you and the sheriff are in the early stages of your relationship."

Really, *really* early. If their so-called relationship were a movie, the previews wouldn't even be showing yet. Seating hadn't even started. The two of them were still standing awkwardly in the corridor with their popcorn, waiting for the theater to be cleaned.

She sighed. "In the unlikely event that I do marry again—far, far in the future, when people are driving hovercrafts instead of cars—I don't think it could be with someone like Cole."

"A sexy responsible guy who's great with kids and beloved by an entire community?"

"Someone in law enforcement. There would be so many painful memories. And I'd worry all the time."

Crystal pursed her lips, looking as if she itched to say more.

In spite of the difficult topic, Kate chuckled. "Out with it, Crys."

"Since I can only imagine what it was like for you and haven't faced anything like it myself, I may not be entitled to an opinion."

"Yet I feel confident you have one."

"Well, I understand why you'd worry," Crystal said, her voice gentle. "How could you not? But…don't you ever watch the news? There are a billion reasons to worry about your loved ones, regardless of their occupations. We can't let that stop us from living. Tragedy happens. Someone could die just—"

"I get your point." Kate held up a hand. "But maybe save the gruesome examples of death and catastrophe for when we're *not* at a birthday party for six-year-olds?"

"Right." Crystal ducked her head, her expression abashed.

The six-year-olds in question had obviously been alerted it was time for gifts and cake. Children began swarming from all directions, putting Kate at the base of an uphill stampede. She joined the migration, glad for an excuse to end the conversation with Crys.

But even though she'd escaped her friend for the moment, Crystal's words stuck with her. *We can't let that stop us from living.* That's not what Kate was doing… was it? She'd met with six potential students and their parents this week and was seeing progress in Luke. Life was good.

Yet she couldn't deny those moments when she yearned for more.

With not one but two guests of honor, there were a ton of presents to unwrap. Kate and Luke gave Mandy a board game that had been one of Luke's favorites when he was younger and Alyssa a pink metronome. Kate was surprised when, after the girls opened those two boxes, Luke turned to the gift table and picked up two very tiny packages in unevenly taped construction paper.

"These are from me," he added.

When Kate saw that he'd given them each a chocolate bar, the same brand he'd stolen, she didn't know whether to laugh or groan. On the other side of the table, Cole's eyebrows shot skyward as he stared the boy down.

Luke grinned. "Bought and paid for with my own money. You can ask Rick."

By unspoken agreement, the girls saved their dad's presents for last. Mandy tore through the packaging and was already putting on her new shin guards by the time Alyssa got to her final gift, a soft stuffed horse with a very sweet expression. She let out a squeal of delight but then mock-scolded, "It was supposed to be a real pony, Daddy."

"You're out of luck on the pony front," Cole told her, "but there is something else at the bottom."

"Sparkly crayons!" Alyssa came out of her seat and ran around the table to hug him. Over the top of her head, Cole's gaze met Kate's. *Thank you*, he mouthed. She wasn't sure she deserved the credit—he'd decided for himself not to go with a creepy doll, and all she'd done was nudge him in an appropriate direction—but the gratitude in his eyes left her feeling tingly and appreciated.

After the gifts, it was time to sing "Happy Birthday to You" and blow out the candles. Then Cole and Kate were planning to duck away and get the next activity ready while the kids ate.

The paintball activity had been Kate's suggestion. It was how her art-teacher friend celebrated the last day of elementary school with graduating fifth graders. Kate hadn't been sure if Cole—or Brody—would agree since the mess factor was intense. But the paint was washable, and neither man had been fazed. Brody said ranch work was always a mess; this would have the added benefit of being colorful. While Kate and Cole prepared the ammunition for the battle, Jazz and Cole's mom would distribute old T-shirts to use as protective smocks.

Cole snagged a paper plate with a slice of cake on it and came toward her. "Want a bite?" he offered.

"No, thanks." His being this close put a quivery feeling in her stomach. Needing to focus on something else, she watched happy kids scarf down cake and ice cream. "So far, the party seems like an unbridled success. If you'll excuse the horse pun."

"The girls are having a blast. I owe you big time. Let me buy you dinner sometime this week?"

Dinner, as in a date? "I… Jazz did just as much work as I did. Possibly more."

"Good point. Brody and Jazz should join us. Will you find out what night works best for them?"

She blinked, startled to find that she suddenly had plans for a double date. But she couldn't think of a reason to say no that didn't sound completely ridiculous. *Then say yes.* "All right." Crystal would be thrilled.

Cole looked pretty happy about it, too. "I can't wait." He grinned down at her, his gorgeous blue eyes crinkling at the corners, melting away the last of her reservations. And most of her ability to think straight.

Weren't they supposed to be doing something right now? Jazz had helped put together a very thorough agenda, and Kate didn't recall a time allotment for "moon over the sheriff."

"Balloons," she blurted.

He nodded. "Let's get to work."

Their version of paintball was to put paint in water balloons. According to the emailed instructions from her friend, if they tried to fill the balloons ahead of time, they risked the paint hardening. Brody had given them use of an outdoor sink behind the barn, and all the supplies were waiting for them there. With a couple of water bottles and funnels, they would fill half the balloons with lime green paint, for Mandy's team, and the other half with bright purple, for Alyssa's. When there were no balloons left to throw, a panel of judges would look at the color splotches on each child to decide which team got the most hits.

There were large rubber buckets on either side of the sink where they would gently deposit the filled balloons. While they worked, Jazz would keep the kids busy with a game of musical chairs. Afterward, children would report to the barn to be divided into teams and collect their ammo. Kate put some paint in an empty bottle, then turned the spigot to add water. Then she capped it and shook vigorously.

"You want to be *very* careful filling the balloons," Kate stressed as she handed Cole one of the funnels. "If you don't use enough water, they won't pop on impact. But too much and—"

"This isn't my first time, sweetheart. Trust me to know what I'm doing."

She responded to the mischief in his tone with a wicked smile. "Even an experienced man can benefit from a few pointers."

"Fair enough." His eyes locked on hers. "But give a guy the chance to show you what he can do first."

The air in her lungs was suddenly too thick to breathe…which maybe accounted for how light-headed she felt. Having played piano for most of her life, she'd developed pretty good manual dexterity. Yet now her fingers were clumsy. It took two attempts to knot the balloon in her hand. She willed herself to concentrate. After half a dozen balloons, she established a cadence. Fill, tie, bucket. Fill, tie, bucket. Fill, tie—*sploosh*.

Startled by the sound, she glanced over at the exact moment Cole swore. A splatter of neon green was dripping from the center of his T-shirt toward the hem. Both of his hands were stained; he looked like the lead suspect in a leprechaun murder. Laughter bubbled up inside her, and she bit her lip, trying in vain to contain it.

His own lips twitched. "Don't you dare say I told you so."

"Wouldn't think of it." Stifled giggles fizzed in the back of her throat like carbonation bubbles. "It would be redundant."

He rinsed his hands in the sink and splashed water at the splotch on his shirt, smearing it into a much bigger mess.

"And petty," she added. "And uncharitable. Hey, Cole?"

He swiveled his head toward her, eyes narrowed in warning.

"Told you so."

"That does it." He cupped a double handful of water and advanced on her.

Laughing uncontrollably, she scrambled back, forgetting about the bucket of balloons behind her.

Cole lunged just as she wobbled. He caught her waist with wet fingers, spinning her toward the side of the barn and away from the paint-filled balloons. "That would have been bad. On the other hand," he said as he righted her, "you would have had the most colorful butt on the ranch."

She'd been enjoying their playfulness, but now, pressed between him and the barn behind her, the moment changed. His gaze dropped to her mouth, and her breath hitched. Hunger that felt at once familiar and alien tightened inside her.

Trying to joke away the nerve-racking desire, she said, "A gentleman wouldn't comment on a woman's butt."

There was no humor in his eyes. "I don't suppose a gentleman would kiss you, either?"

Her brain failed. She couldn't find words for a reply. *So who needs words?* What she needed—what she *wanted*—was the man in front of her.

Lacing her hands behind his neck, she tugged him toward her and stretched up to meet him. His muscles were bunched with deliciously masculine tension, as if he were fighting the urge to take control of their kiss. Her lips brushed his, tentatively. It had been years. She was only half certain she remembered how to do this. Yet she knew Cole was the right man to refresh her memory.

She kissed him again, and her confidence amplified. So did the need spiraling through her.

"Kate." His voice was a ragged murmur. He pulled back slightly, studying her face as if looking for the visual confirmation that this was okay.

She could only imagine what he saw in her expression, but it must have been encouraging. His eyes darkened, and his hand cradled the back of her head. His lips claimed hers in a hot, openmouthed kiss that—

"Daddy?"

Cole recoiled so quickly it was pure luck *he* didn't topple the bucket of water balloons.

Oh, no. No, no, no.

Kate turned her head and saw not just one but both twins. Their matching jaw-dropped gapes made them more identical than Kate had ever seen them.

"You were kissing Miss Kate," Mandy said slowly, as if still trying to process what had happened.

You and me both, kid.

Cole glanced from them to Kate. "We, uh—"

"They're in love!" Alyssa let out a whoop of excitement that debunked the myth of her being the quiet twin. "This is *better* than a pony. Can I be the flower girl at the wedding?"

"What?" Kate's voice came out in a horrified squeak. "Honey, no, it—"

"Why do you get to be the flower girl?" Mandy demanded. "What about me?"

"You don't even like dresses! Weddings are fancy!"

"There is not going to be a wedding," Cole boomed, trying to be heard over all three females.

"Er…everything all right here?" Jazz asked, rounding the barn. "The girls were antsy to know when we could get started, so we were coming to check your progress." Her tone was apologetic. "They ran ahead of me. And then there was yelling."

Kate faked a smile, although her stomach was churning. There were a lot of ways her first kiss in years could have gone wrong; this wasn't one of the ways she'd imagined. "The good news is we have a bunch of balloons ready. Maybe you can start organizing the troops while we finish up the last few."

"Sure." Jazz put an arm around each girl. "C'mon, you two, why don't you go select your teams?" She ushered them to the open pastureland where the battle would take place, and Kate squeezed her eyes shut, wishing she could go back in time.

"I'm not sorry I kissed you," Cole said, sounding a touch defensive.

She cracked one eye open. "Me, neither."

"Really?" A smile lit his face.

"Really. Although," she added wryly, "in retrospect, this might not have been the perfect place for it." Regardless of the damage control he'd have to do—no doubt Alyssa would want to start drawing wedding invitations with her sparkly crayons—today had been a revelation. A part of herself Kate thought might have been lost forever had reawakened with gusto. Whatever else happened, knowing that made her feel more like a whole person than she'd been in a long time.

Cole snickered, and she raised an eyebrow. "What's funny?"

"We have matching blobs." He nodded downward, and she realized that his green paint was now smeared across her top, too. Thank goodness the paint was washable.

"Think we can fill the rest of these without mishap?" she asked.

"I'll be extra careful," he promised. "But…all things considered, I'm glad the other one exploded."

Grinning, she got back to work. Brody and Will began lugging buckets of balloons to where the kids were waiting. They stood in two groups, calling good-natured taunts to each other. Well, mostly good-natured.

Kate was surprised to see Luke sitting off by himself instead of lined up with the others. Granted, he was older than most of the other guests, but she couldn't believe he would pass up the chance to hurl paint-filled water balloons. As Cole explained the rules—and consequences for rule breakers—to the teams, she crossed the grass to her son.

"Hey," she said. "You don't want to participate?"

"Does it *look* like I want to participate?"

She drew back, startled by his hostile tone. "What's wrong?"

He stared at the dirt, nonresponsive.

"I thought you were having fun today," she prodded.

"That was before I saw you sucking face with the sheriff."

Chapter Eight

Gram glanced up from the kitchen table, where she was working a jigsaw puzzle. "How was the...?" Her question trailed off when Luke stomped past the kitchen and into his room. A moment later, the door slammed.

Kate winced, wondering if she should go after him. *And say what?* At the party, she'd taken a stern approach, reminding him that she was his mother and that disagreeing with her actions didn't entitle him to speak to her disrespectfully. Recognizing that his mood was volatile, she'd told Cole they were going to duck out early. The girls had lots of other people to keep them entertained, and paintball had been the last activity on the itinerary anyway. She'd hugged Jazz goodbye and offered to come back later to help with clean up. Jazz had told her it wasn't necessary, that Susan and Crystal were going to pitch in and then the three sisters planned to order pizza and have a movie marathon.

In the car, Kate had softened her approach, acknowledging that she and Luke had never discussed the possibility of her dating and telling him she completely understood if it was a difficult adjustment for him. She'd tried to get him to discuss what he was feeling, but he'd said thinking about it was gross enough without rehashing it aloud. So she'd decided to give him time.

"What was that about?" Gram asked. "He was in a good enough mood when the two of you left."

"Oh, Gram." Tears pricked Kate's eyes. "I don't know what I'm doing."

Her grandmother crossed the room to hug her. "You're not the first mom to feel that way, and you certainly won't be the last. Want me to make you some tea?"

Not if it was caffeinated. She was so keyed up already, caffeine would send her through the roof. "Cole and I kissed. Luke saw it."

"Ah." Her grandmother was silent a moment. "Something stronger than tea, then?"

Kate gave her a watery smile. "Yes, please."

Gram went to a cabinet on the other side of the kitchen and pulled out a bottle of what had been Grandpa Jim's favorite whiskey. She filled a couple of glasses with ice, and the two of them went out to the porch where they could speak without being overheard.

"Thank you." Kate tucked her legs under her on the swing and took a cautious sip of the whiskey. The first swallow burned, but the second one was smooth.

"I have a confession to make," Gram said, taking a nip of her own whiskey. "When Cole announced you'd made plans together, on the very first day you were introduced, I was skeptical. It seemed too fast for my restrained granddaughter, and I thought perhaps I was being…what's the word the kids use? Played! I thought you were playing me. Obviously, I was wrong."

Not so much. "Is 'restrained' a good thing or a bad thing?"

"It's just who you are, darling. You've never been one to make snap decisions."

"Except moving to Cupid's Bow." That moment in her kitchen had felt like an epiphany.

"Maybe that decision was made long before you consciously realized it. No offense to my son, but I always thought you belonged here."

It was true. Cupid's Bow felt more like home than the apartment she and her father had lived in for her entire adolescence. She hoped one day Luke would consider the town home, too. He'd been doing so well until today. How could she blame him for taking the sight of her in a man's arms badly when it had taken her weeks to adjust to the idea?

The two women drank in silence, and Kate almost laughed when Gram refilled their tumblers. At this rate, Luke would see her kissing a man and tottering tipsily through the house in the same day. *Mother of the freaking year.*

Gram stared into the distance, her smile sad.

"Thinking about Grandpa Jim?" Kate asked softly.

"Every day. I knew from the age of twelve he would be the love of my life, and he was. When you told Jim and me that you were engaged, I knew Damon must have been The One. I know how carefully you consider things, and I could hear it in your voice, how happy you were, how *certain*."

Emotion clogged Kate's throat, and she nodded.

"You loved him so much." Her grandmother reached over to clasp her hand. "Nothing will ever take that away or diminish it, not even letting yourself fall in love again."

"Oh, Gram, it's too soon to know whether that will ever happen."

"Really?"

Kate bit her lip. As Gram had pointed out, Kate was guarded with her emotions. If she weren't already falling for Cole—if part of her didn't at least acknowledge it as a possibility—would she have been making out with him at his daughters' party? What had seemed like such a clear decision with his hands on her was muddled now.

"You'll fall in love," her grandmother insisted. "You have a generous heart. Maybe it won't be with the sheriff—although he gets my vote—but you have too much to give to be alone."

"I'm not alone! I have you and Luke."

"Don't be obtuse, dear." Gram stared out across the sprawling yard again, but this time her gaze focused on something specific. "Looks like company."

Kate followed her gaze, watching the car turn onto the farm's dirt road, and her heart jumped. "Cole."

"I'll just leave you to entertain your gentleman caller." It took Gram two tries to successfully rise from the swing. She snickered. "Not as steady on my feet as I was expecting. Good whiskey." She had just disappeared back inside when Cole parked in front of the house.

Oh, boy.

Now what? Last time they'd been on this porch together, Kate had desperately wanted to kiss him. Knowing firsthand what his kisses were like only intensified that ache. But if Luke caught them canoodling twice in one afternoon, he might do something insane like try to hitchhike back to Houston.

"H-hey," she greeted Cole, not standing. She was unsteady enough around him even without the whiskey. "Where are the girls?"

"My mother, who is a saint, should be corralling them into the bathtub even as we speak. Two kids on sugar highs, covered in washable paint." He shook his head. "Suffice to say, they've declared this the most awesome birthday in the world history of birthdays."

"I'm glad."

"Nope. I'm not convinced that's your 'glad' face." He sat in the spot Gram had vacated, brushing a hand over Kate's cheek as he peered at her. The gentle touch was enough to send a small quiver of anticipation through her. "Talk to me, Kate."

"Luke didn't find the day quite as awesome as the girls did." She sighed. "He was trailing after them, coming to offer his assistance with water balloons, too."

"He saw us kiss?" At her nod, Cole's expression turned somber. "That explains your hasty exit."

She'd implied Luke wasn't feeling well when she left but hadn't offered any specifics. "His reaction was a little different than Alyssa's."

"You mean he didn't immediately volunteer to be the ring bearer at our wedding?" He winced at her expression. "Sorry. I thought maybe the situation called for levity."

"I'm not sure what the situation calls for. He was furious on the ride home. He's barely speaking to me."

Cole straightened. "Would it help if I tried talking to him? Man to man, as it were?"

"Um…that may be the worst idea I've ever heard."

He blew out his breath in audible relief. "Praise the

Lord. I mean, I felt I should offer, since I'm responsible for the riff between the two of you, but I don't know what I would have done if you'd said yes. I'm used to talking to five-year-olds who adore me and are easily distracted by sparkly objects. An angry teen is outside my wheelhouse."

She chuckled at the admission. "Wait…what do you mean you're responsible? *I* kissed *you*."

"So you did." His smile was smug and very, very male. "You also agreed to have dinner with me this week. The next night I'm scheduled to be off duty is Tuesday. Coincidentally, Jazz and Brody are available then."

She hesitated, unsure what to say. Part of her couldn't imagine anything more enjoyable than an evening out with her friends and Cole. But was it worth further distressing her son?

"This is becoming an alarmingly long pause," Cole said. "An insecure guy might think you were trying to decide how to get out of dinner."

"I don't know." She stood, unable to meet his gaze. "Maybe going out with you would be a mistake. You didn't see how upset he was when we got home."

Cole followed her, looking mildly annoyed. "You really want to skip over 'maybe he needs some time' straight to 'let's call the whole thing off?' Is this about Luke, or about you?"

"You're a parent. You know making sacrifices comes with the territory."

"True. But you can't live your life jumping through hoops for Luke."

"Actually, he's my son, and I can live *my* life however I choose. And I think it's unbelievably arrogant to give dating advice when, by your own admission, you haven't made time for romance in your life, either."

"There was no one worth the trouble before," he said, his tone softening. "Now there is."

Touched by that declaration, she let him pull her into an apologetic embrace.

"I didn't mean to sound high-handed," he said. "Of course it's your life and you have to make the decisions you feel are best. But kids are resilient. Don't you think he'll get used to the idea?"

"I just relocated him from the only home he's ever known. He's already having to adjust to a lot."

Cole released her. His frustration was evident on his face, but his voice was contrite. "I told you I was a patient man, yet here I am pushing. I just… There's something powerful between us, Kate, and I'd like to see where it takes us."

After today, she couldn't deny the escalating attraction they shared. It was where that attraction would lead that gave her pause. If dinner Tuesday were only some people getting together to eat, she'd go in a heartbeat. Children rarely needed therapy because their mothers went out for hickory-smoked ribs. But by Cole's own admission, a date with him would be more than that. It would be another step forward on a perilous road to an unknown destination.

Then again, how could she ever expect her son to grow accustomed to their moving forward if she herself couldn't get comfortable with the idea? She turned away, considering. The memory of kissing Cole was vivid, but not just the physical part. She was struck by that moment when he'd paused, holding in check his own desires to make sure it was really what she wanted.

There'd been so much tender concern in his gaze that it made her ache.

"Okay," she said, quickly before she could change her mind. Again.

"You'll have dinner with me Tuesday?" His voice was nine parts joy, one part disbelief.

She nodded. "It's a date."

WHEN LUKE HAD awakened the first time on Sunday to morning sunlight filling his room, he'd rolled over and gone back to sleep. But now it was past noon. He kept his eyes tightly closed, willing himself back into the refuge of sleep, but it was pointless. He wasn't tired.

He was, however, starving. And he had to go to the bathroom.

Sitting up, he eyed his closed door, the much-needed barrier between him and the rest of the world. *I do not want to go out there.*

But remaining in his sanctuary was no guarantee that he wouldn't have to face his mom. Eventually, she would knock and try to talk to him. As if he had anything to say besides "yuck." What the hell was wrong with her? She'd been at a birthday party for little kids. Nobody needed to see *that*.

Except he couldn't seem to unsee it. The image of her macking on the sheriff had plagued him all night long.

Ever since they'd left the ranch yesterday, Luke had been trying to remember a specific instance of his mom and dad kissing. He couldn't do it. Oh, he knew he'd seen them kiss, but he couldn't pinpoint an actual, individual memory. And it seemed wrong that he couldn't remember his dad kissing her but now he was stuck with a visual of some other guy doing it.

Through the door, he heard the house phone ring and his mom's muffled voice as she answered. Good. Maybe he could run to the bathroom, then snag some food to bring back to his room while she was distracted. Yet he'd no sooner grabbed a sleeve of crackers from the pantry when his mother came toward him with the cordless phone.

She handed it to him. "It's Sarah."

He groaned at the ambush. Last night, he hadn't felt like answering any of his friend's texts, but that hadn't dissuaded her from sending them. So he'd turned off his phone.

"Hello?" he snapped.

There was a pause. "Hi to you, too, Grumpy."

"What do you want?"

"My cousin is coming to visit, and my brother and I are trying to plan a couple of things to do while he's in town so he won't be bored silly. We'll probably go to a matinee tomorrow." She hesitated. "I thought... well, would you like to come with us?"

"No." He didn't want to deal with people. Not his mom, not Sarah, not anyone.

From across the kitchen, where she was making a sandwich, his mother frowned at his tone. Obviously she thought he was being rude. Well, eavesdropping was rude, too.

"Are you gonna be online later?" Sarah asked, a little wobble in her voice. "Because I just got the code for a new DLC and—"

"I don't want to play or go to the movie. And I don't want to talk to you! Take the hint already."

She gasped. "You don't have to be a jerk about it." Then she hung up.

Crap. Sarah was right. He *had* been a jerk. Knowing he'd hurt her feelings made him feel like he'd swallowed live goldfish and they were wriggling through his gut. Why couldn't she have left him alone? Now he'd probably lost his only friend in this stupid town.

He remembered the day he'd drawn that horse picture for Aly. *"I guess you can be my friend."* Aly was a cute kid, but he didn't want to see her again. How could he be around her without thinking about her dad with his mom?

His mother was like Bobby Rowe. That comparison would probably make her head explode, but Bobby had a thing for redheads. Every girl Bobby had ever talked about or asked to a school dance had red hair. Maybe Luke's mom had a thing for policemen. That was one explanation for why she'd be all over some guy she'd only known a few weeks.

"Luke." His mom set the sandwich on the table in front of him. "You were really unkind to her. I'm disappointed in you."

That was nothing new. "She should have got a clue when I didn't respond to her texts," he muttered.

"Don't blame her for your actions." She sat in the chair next to him. "And don't blame her for mine, either. I know you're upset that Cole and I—"

"Can we not talk about that?" He resisted the urge to clap his hands over his ears, but just barely.

"We'll need to eventually, because I'm seeing him again. For dinner on Tuesday. I realize this can't be easy for you, but—"

"I'm not hungry." He shoved the sandwich away.

He noticed her jaw tighten, but she didn't make him eat. "I have two piano students coming today, and I don't need you snarling at them. Maybe it would be best if you spent the afternoon in your room."

Fine by me.

Stalking down the hallway, he thought he heard a sniff behind him, but he ignored it. Just as he ignored his own sniffles as he shut his door once more.

ON MONDAY MORNING, Kate went on a cleaning frenzy fueled by nervous energy. She had only one piano student scheduled for that afternoon—Alyssa Trent—and she was worried about how the lesson would go. Had Cole successfully convinced his daughters that he and Kate weren't planning to head down the aisle?

As Kate stowed the furniture polish and cleaning rag back under the kitchen sink, she comforted herself with the reminder that at least Cole wouldn't be the one bringing his daughter. It seemed too soon for him and Luke to be under the same roof. Cole was working today, and he'd left a message that his mother would drive Alyssa to the farm. Frankly, Kate wasn't sure how her son would act toward Alyssa, either, but since Gram was at quilting club, Kate didn't have an easy way to get Luke out of the house. *If only he'd accepted Sarah's invitation to the movies.*

Kate's heart hurt for the girl, whose overtures of friendship had been so adamantly rebuffed. She hated that Luke was sabotaging himself, but this wasn't the first time he'd fallen into self-destructive behavior when upset. She found herself grateful that no man had attracted her attention back in Houston; she could only imagine the trouble Luke would be in right now if he were still hanging out with Bobby and his cohorts.

Patch barked cheerfully, letting her know they had company, and Kate reached the front door at the same time Mrs. Trent did.

Kate waved the woman and her granddaughter inside. "Nice to see you both again."

Rather than returning Kate's smile, Alyssa hopped from one foot to the other, her face tense. "I hafta use the bathroom, Miss Kate."

"Right down the hall."

As the girl hurried away, Gayle said, "Sorry about that. I shouldn't have let her order the large soda with lunch."

"No problem. She's my only student today, so if we start a few minutes late, I can make up the time. Do you want to sit in on the lesson, or wait in the living room? You're welcome to watch television if you like."

"I believe I'll curl up on the sofa and read if you don't mind." She pulled a book out of her purse. "I'm halfway through a great mystery and can't wait to find out who the killer is."

Kate smiled noncommittally. Personally, she stayed away from mysteries and thrillers. She hated the reminder that bad guys were out there. In the case of her husband's killer, he'd been caught and sentenced, but seeing justice served had done nothing to bring Damon back to her.

"You don't like books?" Gayle asked as she settled on the couch.

"Oh, I love to read. The darker stuff just isn't for me. I prefer laughing my way through a book and knowing there's a happy ending."

"So, you like romances. I shouldn't be surprised." Gayle grinned. "According to my granddaughters, you're *definitely* a fan of romance."

Embarrassment heated Kate's face. "I, uh…"

"No need to feel bashful. I'm thrilled my son is finally falling for a good woman. And both the girls have taken a shine to you."

Kate glanced down the hallway, willing Alyssa to return. Immediately. "Thank you. But…"

Gayle arched an eyebrow. "Uh-oh. Don't tell me you're planning to break his heart."

How invested was Cole's heart? Kate knew his mom had interfered in his love life before, and she wouldn't put it past the well-meaning woman to exaggerate.

"I don't think people ever really plan for that," Kate said. Sometimes it just happened. It was impossible to know the future. "Can I ask you a personal question?"

"Yes, especially if it's about Cole. I have many adorable stories about his childhood."

Kate grinned, charmed by the mental image of Cole as a little boy, with those laser-bright blue eyes. "Maybe another time." She looked down the hall, verifying that the bathroom door was still closed, then lowered her voice. "You're the mother of a sheriff and a fireman, both jobs that include a lot of inherent risk. Don't you worry about them constantly?"

"You're a mom yourself, so you know the answer to that. Of course I worry. We all worry about our children, even those who grow up to be accountants or retail cashiers."

Kate supposed that was true.

"My pride in my boys is stronger than my fear. Jace, the youngest, makes me want to pull my hair out sometimes, but even he is dependable in an emergency and quick to help others. I consider my sons modern-day heroes. They're noble and kind." She sighed. "But not very lucky in love. I'm hoping that will change."

Kate bit her lip. "Cole and his brothers are great guys. I'm sure they'll find women who see that." She just didn't know yet if she would be one of those women.

GRAM LEANED BACK in her armchair, temporarily abandoning the knitting she'd been doing. "When I was a girl, our house had a basement and sometimes Mama or Daddy would send me down the stairs to fetch something. I never told them, but I was *terrified* of that basement, even up 'til I was sixteen. I only mention it now because you're looking down the hall at Luke's door the way I used to eye that basement door. What are you afraid of—that he's going to come busting out of that room, wild-eyed and screaming when Cole picks you up for dinner?"

Maybe. Kate sat on the very edge of the sofa, trying not to wrinkle the sundress she'd chosen. "I don't know what I'm afraid of." Parenting failures, love, loss, the uncertainty of the future. "A little bit of everything, I guess."

Gram peered over the rims of her glasses. "Well, stop it."

Kate couldn't help chuckling at the command. *If only it were that simple.* "I hope Luke doesn't give you any trouble while I'm gone."

"Frankly, I'd be surprised if he even shows his face. Been keeping to himself a lot the last few days."

Kate nodded. She'd overheard him trying to talk

to Sarah through the gaming headphones, but apparently his friend wasn't ready to forgive him. Luke had logged off, dejected. Kate thought it might be a nice gesture for him to do something "in real life" with her, so that Sarah knew he saw her as a real friend and not just someone to campaign with when he needed help defeating a level. Kate had suggested as much, but he'd simply glared. Her son wasn't particularly receptive to her advice right now.

Patch ran to the front door with a bark and a wagging tail, and Kate's stomach felt the exact same way it had the single time she'd allowed Damon and Luke to talk her into riding a roller coaster with an upside down loop. While she took a deep, calming breath, Gram answered the door.

"Sheriff." Gram's tone was rich with humor. "I expect you to have her back at a reasonable hour. It's a weeknight, after all."

Cole grinned. "Yes, ma'am." Then his gaze shifted to Kate. "You look fantastic."

The time she'd taken with her hair and makeup had definitely been worth it. At the girls' party, Jazz had given her an undeniably fashionable appearance, but that look hadn't really been Kate. She was glad Cole was equally impressed with the real her. "Thank you. So do you." But then, he always did.

He held out his hand, and as she walked toward him, her nerves evaporated. There was nowhere she'd rather be tonight than in this man's company. "Don't worry, Mrs. Denby," he told Gram, "I won't keep her out past curfew."

Once they were on the other side of the door, Cole surprised Kate by pulling her closer for a quick kiss hello. "I couldn't wait until the end of the evening to do that," he said.

She was glad he hadn't, but couldn't resist teasing him anyway. "Are you also the kind of person who eats dessert first?"

His gaze dipped from hers, traveling the length of her body and back. "If dessert looked as delectable as you? Hell yes."

Warmth filled her, and the way he gallantly opened her car door for her only amplified it.

There was a police radio in Cole's car, but he turned it off as he slid into the driver's seat. "They can reach me on my cell if there's a real emergency," he said. "Besides..."

Although he didn't finish his sentence, she could guess from his expression what he was thinking. He wanted to protect her—and protect their date—from reminders of his job. She sighed, recalling his mother's words from yesterday. Cole was noble and heroic. Kate would never want to change that about him. Being sheriff was a big part of his life. It must sting to feel as though he had to tiptoe around it, never discussing his job the way normal couples did on normal dates.

If she was going to attempt dating him, she should commit to it, not settle for a half-ass effort. "So what made you decide to go into police work?" she asked. "Family member on the force? The desire to help citizens in a crisis or return stolen purses to damsels in distress?"

At first, she thought his pause was because she'd surprised him with the question. After a moment, it became clear he was stalling on purpose. "I don't think I want to tell you. The answer makes me a lot less cool."

She laughed. "We're single parents. There are plenty of things that make our lives uncool. If it makes you feel any better, it's not like I expected this evening to end with me wearing your leather jacket and riding home on the back of your motorcycle."

"I was inspired to be a cop because of a TV show."

"That's not embarrassing. Police shows are a television legacy."

"Miranda's Rights," he said.

It took her a moment to place the name. "The old soap opera?"

"It was my mom's favorite when I was little. She had it on every afternoon, and I thought Miranda had a really exciting life. One season, she was abducted by aliens! Life around here was pretty dull, in comparison. The entire time I was growing up, I did not meet one person who suffered from amnesia or discovered they have an evil twin."

Kate snorted with laughter. "That's the reason you wanted to become a cop? So you could experience aliens and amnesia?"

"I was young and impressionable. And you are a very cruel woman, prying for personal secrets just so you can make fun of me."

"Sorry," she lied, still laughing. "I just wasn't expecting an answer like that. Now it makes me curious about those stories your mom offered to share yesterday. I'm sincerely hoping that you used to pretend to be your own evil twin. Or that you feigned amnesia to get out of a math test or something."

"You know, I was just thinking last month that I'd love to send my parents on a cruise. A long, *long* cruise, far away from beautiful blondes looking to mock me."

He paused, then added slyly, "Maybe I should ask your grandmother for intriguing stories about your childhood."

That sobered her quickly. "Truce? I never bring up your affinity for cheesy soap operas, and you don't interrogate Gram."

"I don't know." He smirked. "Now you have me curious."

Kate had always loved music and grew up with a tendency to sing no matter where she was. Unfortunately, as a child, she hadn't always understood the lyrics of certain songs she caught on the radio, which had led to more than one inappropriate public concert. She remembered Gram hustling her out of a grocery store one day after a woman in frozen foods stared at Kate in horror.

"Change of subject," she declared. "Where are we going to eat?" Culinary selections in Cupid's Bow were limited. The food was all good, but there weren't many choices.

"Actually, I'm taking us to an Italian place a couple of towns over. I hope Jazz and Brody don't have any trouble finding it. After all the work the three of you did giving my daughters an amazing birthday, I wanted to do something special in return. Plus, the long drive gives you and me more time together." He slanted her an avid look that made her pulse race, then smiled sheepishly. "I may also have been motivated by the fact that Becca Johnston is hosting a volunteer dinner at my favorite in-town restaurant."

Kate grinned. "Well, at least you're man enough to admit you're avoiding her. Did you give her an answer on the bachelor auction yet?"

"Yeah, I caved. I sent an email agreeing to participate but am dodging her suggestions that we get together to discuss specifics in person. Kate, I know it's presumptuous to ask you to bid, but…please, please don't let that woman get me."

"You realize that in order to stop her, I'd probably need to take out a mortgage on the farm?"

"I will pay you back every dime. Who needs savings? For all I know, my girls won't want to go to college anyway. Maybe they'll take after their Uncle Jace."

She would have laughed if she hadn't spent so many sleepless nights fretting over her own kid's future. She'd invested some of the life-insurance money to help pay for college, but more than once, she questioned whether he'd even be accepted anywhere. University enrollment would require improved grades and fewer disciplinary problems. Being suspended from school didn't look good on an application.

"Auction aside," Cole said, "you are planning to visit the festival, right?"

"Isn't it mandatory for all Cupid's Bow citizens?" she teased. "I've been under the impression that one would be run out of town for skipping it."

"Correct. Unless you have a note from the doctor excusing you."

"I used to go every summer with my grandparents. I'm looking forward to it." The festival would kick off next Friday. Kate had already agreed to join Gram for a couple of volunteer events.

"I'll be working in an official capacity for most of festival weekend," Cole said, "but I'm supposed to have a few hours free Sunday afternoon. Do you think maybe we could go together? All of us, the kids, too."

Oh, boy. She could just imagine the sneer on Luke's face when she informed him of that plan. As his mom, she could force him to go. But it was difficult to force someone to have a good time. The last thing she wanted was for his dour attitude to ruin the girls' fun. And the girls presented an entirely different problem. Would seeing Luke and Kate together only encourage their dreams of getting a stepmom?

Part of her yearned to say yes, but she couldn't bring herself to agree without further consideration. Instead she joked, "Let me get this straight—you want me to commit to being your date for the festival *and* to bidding on you for yet another date? That's a lot of investment on my part when we've barely even started our first date. What if tonight's a disaster?"

He laughed. "You don't have to give me your answer yet. I can wait. But, for the record? Tonight's going to be wonderful."

Chapter Nine

Kate was having the time of her life. The mushroom ravioli she'd ordered had been well worth the drive, the dinner conversation was punctuated with frequent laughter and Cole somehow made her feel like the most beautiful woman in the room, despite the fact that she was seated across from a woman who, up until Christmas, had been a professional model. *And to think you almost told him no when he asked you out.* She leaned against the high-backed booth with a happy sigh. *New policy. From now on, always tell Cole yes.*

A blush climbed her cheeks as she considered situations far racier than dinner.

"Kate?" Jazz tilted her head, studying her from the other side of the candlelit table. "You okay? You look flushed."

Turning toward her, Cole tucked her hair back to study her face. Even that slight touch sent tingles up her spine. For the past hour and a half, they'd been in repeated contact. He'd held hands with her, their legs brushed beneath the table, and at one point when the restaurant's air-conditioning had kicked on, he'd seized the opportunity to put his arm around her and pull her close because she "looked cold."

"Everything all right?" he asked softly.

The heat she'd been feeling intensified. "Must be the wine I had." Or the fact that she hadn't been able to stop thinking about kissing him again all night. It was ironic that the more fun she had on their double date, the more she couldn't wait to leave and get him alone. He was an undeniably attractive man, but his attentiveness to her was even more arousing than his physical appearance.

"Want me to catch the waitress's attention and get you another glass of ice water?" He scanned the dining area, pausing to nod hello to a man approaching their table.

"Evenin', Sheriff." The stranger was tall and handsome. He held a black cowboy hat in his hand, and his sun-streaked hair was attractively scruffy, as was the hint of beard that shadowed his jaw. "Brody."

Brody shook the man's hand. "Jarrett. You know Jasmine Tucker and Kate Sullivan?"

The man's smile widened. "Afraid I haven't had the pleasure. Jarrett Ross. Are you ladies from Cupid's Bow, too?"

Jazz nodded. "Cole promised the food would be worth the extra drive. He's obviously not the only one who feels that way." The dining room was packed.

"This place stays busy," Jarrett agreed. He held up one of the buzzers used to signal when a table was ready. "My date and I are hoping we'll have time to eat and still catch a movie after this."

"I knew there had to be a date somewhere," Brody said. "With you, there's always a pretty woman involved."

"Look who's talking," Jarrett said with a wink in Jasmine's direction. "Tiffani's in the ladies' room."

Brody and Jarrett chatted about ranching business for a few minutes. Kate liked horses, but not enough to focus on the conversation with fantasies of Cole crowding her thoughts. He caught her watching him, and grinned. His hand dropped below the table to caress her thigh. Despite the fabric of her dress and the linen napkin she had across her lap, the slow stroke of his thumb felt as intimate as if he were touching bare skin. If she were alone with him right now...

"Oh, that's us." The pager in Jarrett's hand flashed red. "You guys enjoy the rest of your evening. I'm sure I'll run into you at the Watermelon Festival." He scowled. "Somehow Becca Johnston convinced me that because of the equine therapy work I do with disabled children, I have to be part of her 'heroes' auction. That woman is frighteningly persuasive."

As he walked away, Cole added, "Or just frightening, period."

Jazz craned her head to watch Jarrett go. "He'll have no trouble raising bids. You know I love you, Brody, but speaking on a completely objective level as someone whose former career centered around the human form...whoa."

Kate laughed, temporarily distracted enough from lusting after Cole that she finally recognized Jarrett's name. "Wait, *he's* the rodeo cowboy Gram's friend was trying to set me up with?"

Cole poked her in the shoulder with his index finger. "Don't even think about it. You are currently unavailable." Though his tone was playful, there was a note of possessiveness she found thrilling.

"Don't worry, I don't want anyone but you."

His eyes darkened, and she knew that if they weren't sitting in a crowded restaurant right now, he'd be kissing her breathless.

"Aww." Jazz had her chin propped on her fist, grinning at them as if she were watching a favorite romantic movie. "Nothing makes me happier than seeing two terrific people fall in—"

Bracing herself for the impact of the word *love*, Kate's entire body stiffened. Noticing, Cole cut off Jazz's sentence. "Yeah, seems like Cupid's Bow is sure getting a workout lately," he said, putting enough jocular emphasis on the pun to make the other couple groan.

For her part, Kate wanted to hug him in gratitude. She hoped her involuntary reaction hadn't hurt his feelings, but she deeply appreciated his sensitivity. There was no pretending they hadn't entered a relationship, whether she'd been looking for one or not, but to admit she might be falling in love with him? She wasn't ready to jump off that cliff.

"How did Cupid's Bow get its name anyway?" Jazz asked. "Anyone know?"

"Topography," Cole said. "When you look at a map, the town border is roughly bow-shaped."

Brody chuckled. "Guess Cupid's Bow sounded friendlier than Archery or Longbow, Texas. Definitely more tourist appeal than Death by Arrow, Texas."

Kate managed a laugh along with the others, but her heart wasn't in it. Just because an arrow was shot by Cupid didn't make it any less dangerous.

As FAR AS Cole could tell, the evening had lived up to his initial promise of being wonderful. Frankly, it had been a gamble to make that boast. Kate's misgivings about dating were completely understandable. But since she was uncertain, he'd decided he just had to be confident enough for both of them. It had worked pretty well.

The only misstep at dinner had been that moment when she'd almost panicked over Jazz's careless phrasing. As close as he'd been sitting to Kate, he'd imagined he could actually feel the pounding of her pulse. She'd gone momentarily wild-eyed. But after he changed the subject, she'd eventually relaxed again.

Still, she was a lot quieter during the drive back to her grandmother's farm than she had been on the way to the restaurant. Maybe she was sleepy and pleasantly mellow from a rich dinner and two glasses of wine. If she were regretting their date, she would be leaning away from him, not angled in his direction and holding his hand while he drove.

Perhaps the lull in conversation was simply because she was enjoying the music from the radio. Her fingers periodically tapped along with the beat, moving across his knuckles in unconscious rhythm. As he turned onto the dirt road that marked Denby property, Kate reached for the volume button, humming softly as an acoustic ballad began.

"I love this song," she said.

Cole had been wishing he could prolong their time alone—once he pulled up in front of the farmhouse, there was a possibility their goodbyes would be monitored by Joan. Or, worse, Luke. Kate's statement gave him the excuse he'd needed. He put the car in Park and hit the button to lower the windows so that the music floated out into the night. Then he removed his seat-belt and got out of the car. She regarded him curiously.

He came around the other side and opened her door, holding out one hand. "Dance with me?"

She hesitated only a second, then reached over to bump up the volume again. A poignant melody combined with the drowsy pulse of tree frogs and crickets. Kate wrapped her arms around his neck and let him pull her much closer than would have been appropriate at the local dance hall. It felt indescribably good to have her against him. Too good. As they swayed together, his body responded with the full force of desire he'd tried to temper all evening. His senses had been filled with her, the sound of her laugh, the scent of her shampoo, the lushness of her curves as his body brushed hers.

Standing this close, there was no way to hide the effect she had on him, so he owned up to it instead, hoping the feeling was mutual. "You are a very sexy woman. It's been driving me crazy all night, in the best possible way." He held his breath, waiting to follow her lead. If she shied away—

"Cole?" Her fingers skated up the sensitive nape of his neck and threaded through his hair. "Kiss me."

He was eager to oblige, yet savored the moment, first pressing a kiss to the delicate skin beneath her ear, then dotting his way across her cheek. When his mouth reached hers, she melted in his arms, her lips parted in invitation. His tongue slid across hers, and he nearly groaned with pleasure. Their kiss went from explorative to hungry, his hand tangled in the soft cotton of her dress as he crushed her against him.

The billions of stars twinkling in the summer sky

were nothing compared to the stars he saw when Kate kissed him. His need for her made him feverish, reckless. The last time he'd considered trying to seduce a woman in the back seat of a car, he'd been in high school. Perhaps if he had a blanket or a coat to spread on the ground...

With great reluctance, he broke their kiss, needing a moment to catch his breath. And rein in his libido. It wasn't until he released her that he realized not only was a different song playing, it was fading to its last notes.

"That was..." She touched a finger to her bottom lip, her expression awestruck. The look in her eyes was a greater stroke to his ego than every compliment he'd heard his entire life, added together.

His laugh had a rough, strangled quality to it. "Keep looking at me like that, and I might forget that the gentlemanly thing to do is to take you to your front door and call it a night."

She inhaled deeply, and he couldn't help but admire the swell of her breasts at the neckline of her dress. "Part of me doesn't want to call it a night."

Which meant that part of her *did*. Shoring up his self-discipline, he stepped away from her. Too bad it wasn't thirty degrees cooler. Chilly evening air would help him clear his head.

It was a pretty night, though, and he was greedy for more time with her. "Want to walk from here?" he asked.

"Sure."

He turned off the car, locked it and pocketed the keys. Then he twined his fingers through hers and they headed down the informal, winding driveway that cut through the pasture. Ahead, lights shone through the front windows of the farmhouse. Was her grandmother waiting inside to gently interrogate Kate about their evening? If he'd left the twins with his mother, he knew Gayle would pepper him with questions the second he crossed over the threshold. Instead, he'd hired a sitter and hadn't told his mom or his daughters about his date. If Kate agreed to come with him and the girls to the festival next Sunday, Alyssa and Mandy would have proof soon enough that he was seeing her. If she said no, he didn't want them to be disappointed.

And how will you *handle it if she says no?* Disappointment would be too mild a word to cover his feelings if Kate didn't want to see him again.

"I have a confession to make," he said.

"Please tell me it involves another soap opera from the eighties," she teased. "Because that would make my night."

"Brat," he grumbled affectionately. "No, I was going to say that, as much as I enjoyed tonight, I'm eager to see you again when I don't have to share you with anyone else."

She slanted him a look that was difficult to read in the dark. "I'd like that."

"Maybe I could cook you dinner." The offer surprised him. When was the last time he'd cooked for a woman? "I'm sure Mom would be willing to keep the girls at her place for a few hours." It would mean admitting to his mother what his plans were, but he was willing to endure one of his mom's inquisitions in order to get unchaperoned time with Kate.

"Sounds wonderful."

"I'll check my schedule and call you so we can figure out a time." He was relieved that he sounded normal and not like a lovesick fool who was already counting the hours until he could be with her again.

KATE WAS AT the desk in her room, checking email on her laptop when the phone rang late Thursday morning. Since she knew Gram was in the house, she ignored it and started typing her response to the high school drama teacher, who'd written to ask if Kate offered voice lessons. The high school would be putting on a musical in the fall, and the teacher thought it might be wise to call in reinforcements for helping the teens prepare.

"Katie?" Gram knocked on the bedroom door. "Phone for you, dear."

Was Cole calling to cancel their dinner date this evening? It was a completely irrational thought—she had no reason to expect him to bail—but she'd been thinking about tonight so much, it was the first thing that occurred to her. When she'd accepted his invitation, she hadn't expected their next date to be quite so soon. But as he'd explained when he phoned yesterday, between duty at the county courthouse and the upcoming festival, his schedule was pretty packed for the next week and a half.

She opened her door. "Thanks, Gram." She raised the receiver to her ear, torn between fierce hope that Cole's plans hadn't changed and the niggling, cowardly hope that he *did* need to postpone. Based on how he'd kissed her the last time he'd seen her—and how she'd kissed him back—she knew their physical relationship was escalating. Was she ready for that? "Hello?"

"Hi, Kate. I hate to do this to you, but I need to cancel. Monica's got a bad summer cold."

Kate blinked. "Mrs. Abernathy?"

"Yes. Sorry, I shouldn't have assumed your grandmother told you who was calling. I'm afraid Monica won't be able to make it this afternoon."

"Oh." Relief that it wasn't Cole on the phone flooded her, overwhelming her so completely that it took a moment to collect her thoughts. "I'm sorry to hear she isn't feeling well. Just call me back when she's doing better, and we'll schedule a makeup lesson."

"Thanks for understanding. I'll talk to you soon."

As Kate disconnected the call, she was struck by the revelation of how much she wanted Cole. The sheer joy that had filled her when she'd realized it wasn't him, that he wasn't abandoning their plans, was staggering. To some extent, it was even liberating. Yet, now that she'd confirmed how much the night ahead meant to her, the unoccupied hours between then and now yawned in a void, the perfect incubation conditions for self-doubt.

In dire need of moral support, she dialed Crystal's number, expelling a pent up breath when her friend answered. "Hey, it's Kate. You know how we've been saying we should get Luke and Noah together? By any chance, could we do that today? I'm having dinner with Cole tonight, and I desperately need to be distracted so I don't spend the next seven hours fixating."

"Dinner, again?" Crystal whistled. "Jazz said she and Brody just went out with you guys. Two dates in one week—tell me again how this isn't serious?"

I can't. Not when she'd spent the majority of her waking hours obsessing over their last date, replaying his kisses in her mind. She'd even downloaded that ballad they'd danced to, had listened to it so often in the last day and a half that Luke and Gram were beginning to look at her strangely. "So…do you have some time this afternoon?"

"Well. I did have scintillating plans to do laundry— you wouldn't believe the amount of clothes five kids go through—and clean out my refrigerator. Obviously, I'll be brokenhearted to have to reschedule all that, but since it's for you…"

After a few more minutes of discussion, they decided to feed their respective children early lunches, then meet at the community pool. Kate knocked on the door to Luke's room to alert him to the day's agenda. He didn't react with anything as drastic as a smile, but he nodded quickly. He was probably getting cabin fever hanging around the farm.

He was almost cordial during lunch. Though she hated to jeopardize that progress, it was time to tell Luke about her plans to go to the festival with Cole. She broached the subject on the way to the pool, while he was buckled into the passenger seat and couldn't retreat to his room.

"Luke, you know the Watermelon Festival is coming up, right?"

"Duh. Everyone's been talking about it since we got here. These people take watermelon *really* seriously."

That made her laugh. "The festival is a town tradition and, believe it or not, a huge tourism draw. I was planning on taking you."

He shrugged. "'Kay."

"It's a four-day event and we don't have to go every day, although Gram mentioned there are some stations that could use a little extra volunteer help. But on Sunday, the last day…" She cast him a nervous glance, unsure how he'd react. "The sheriff and his daughters asked us to join them. We could all go together."

His expression tightened. "Don't you two get sick of each other? You're going out with him *again* tonight and I haven't complained about how gross that is. But that doesn't mean I want to be with you on one of your dates! That I want to see…"

"Luke—"

"I don't want to talk about it."

"Tough." She'd tried to be patient, but they couldn't resolve anything with him holed up in his room. Gram had coaxed him out to earn some allowance with farm chores, but he'd avoided interacting with Kate. "We have to do plenty of things in life we don't want to do." Like saying goodbye to loved ones. Like figuring out how to move on, no matter how painful or daunting that was.

Of course, her insistence that they discuss the issue was funny given that she still didn't know exactly what to say. She kept it basic. "Cole is a very nice man. I'd like for you to get along with him."

He shot her a look that made it clear he considered this an insane request. "You never liked my friend Bobby. I don't have to like your *friend*, either."

She silently counted to ten. "Maybe that will come in time. You do have to be civil, though. That's nonnegotiable. We're joining him and the girls next Sunday, at least for an hour or two. The twins look up to you. Can you try to leave the attitude at home?"

"We don't have a home," he said under his breath.

So much for her hope that he was warming up to

life in Cupid's Bow. She thought wistfully of his buoyant mood after he'd volunteered at the hospital with Rick. Then he'd befriended Sarah. He'd been making strides in the right direction. *Until he saw you and Cole kissing.* Knowing what a setback that had been for her son, how could she justify going through with her date tonight?

Cole's words on Gram's porch came back to her. *You can't live your life jumping through hoops for Luke.* For so long, it had felt as if she weren't living life at all. At best, she'd been coping, merely surviving from one day to the next. She'd shown up at work, taught her students songs and gone home to Luke in the evenings, usually with dread over the latest notes from his teachers. There hadn't been anything she'd looked forward to, nothing she'd anticipated with joy.

Even the nervous fear that gripped her when she pondered her feelings for Cole was preferable to that bleak numbness.

"Just promise me, Luke, that you won't be insufferable at the festival. Don't be rude to Cole or his daughters."

"Fine."

Having extracted that agreement, no matter how surly, she decided to count this conversation as a win. Or at least as a strategic advance in the ongoing battle of motherhood. Deciding to be a gracious victor, she turned on the radio and left him in peace for the rest of the ride.

When they reached the pool and she spotted Crystal unloading five children and all their swim paraphernalia from a minivan, Kate felt a twinge of guilt.

"Thank you so much for meeting me," she said as

she leaned in the van to help unfasten a one-year-old from a car seat. "I didn't think about how challenging it must be for you to make spontaneous plans."

"Don't mention it," Crystal said. "The kids love to come. It's early enough that I could even bring the little ones and they will absolutely *crash* later. Come naptime, I'll be singing your praises while I indulge in some peace and quiet."

"All the same, as far as I'm concerned, you're a superhero." Kate felt as if she had her hands full with *one* child, and Crys managed five? It was odd to think that their oldest kids were roughly the same ages. Crys had a child in middle school, one in elementary school, one in preschool and two toddlers. Starting all over with babies at this point felt incomprehensible.

But what about stepchildren? The thought came totally out of the blue. Kate's kneejerk reaction was instant denial, but didn't she know better than most that there was no way to know what the future held? That was true of the blessings as well as the tragedies.

Between the two adults and the assistance of the older kids, they herded the small children and a metric ton of towels, floatation devices, face masks and dive toys onto the patio area. After making sure everyone was adequately covered in sunscreen, Crystal and Kate agreed that the oldest kids could go to the main pool. Meanwhile, they took the twin toddlers and the five-year-old to a soft-surfaced fountain play area where they could run squealing through cooling jets of water.

"You sure *you* put on enough sunscreen?" Crystal asked Kate with exaggerated concern. "I'd hate for you to get sunburned before your big date. Nothing kills a moment like a man reaching for you and you responding with 'ow!'"

"Hey!" Kate cupped her hand in a bubbling spray and splashed her friend. "You're supposed to be distracting me from the big date, remember? Not tormenting me about it."

"Oh, please." Crystal put her hands on her hips. "Other people are willingly babysitting your respective kids so you can have a child-free evening and the incredibly hot sheriff is making you a home-cooked meal. Which part of that is ammunition for torment?"

Kate made a mental note to try to babysit for Crystal sometime soon; surely she and her husband could use the time to reconnect. "No, it all sounds heavenly. Except...without the angelic, saintly behavior."

"Ah, now that sounds promising! Got naughty plans?" Crystal waggled her eyebrows. "The man does own handcuffs."

Kate blushed so dramatically she probably did look sunburned to anyone looking her way. "Not helping, you lunatic!"

Crystal giggled, and her boys wanted to get in on the fun. Splashing and laughter commenced. Kate was holding one of the twins, swooping him toward his mom in threatening pursuit when she caught sight of her own son standing by the pool. Although it was difficult to be certain from this distance, it looked as if he was talking to Sarah Pemberton. Had Luke repaired his friendship after hurting the girl's feelings? Maybe Sarah had just needed a little time to forgive him—just as Luke needed time to accept his mom's relationship with Cole.

The anxiety that had been plaguing her all day

suddenly seemed ridiculous. Stress was no match for standing in the sunlight, surrounded by laughing children.

A few minutes later, Luke raced over to the kiddie area. "Mom! Can I go out with Sarah and her brother and her cousin tonight? Her brother and cousin are both old enough to drive. They want to see a movie and get a burger afterward. I have plenty of allowance saved up to pay," he added when she didn't immediately agree.

Money hadn't been her chief concern, although she was glad he'd volunteered to spend his own cash. Ideally, she'd be home to both vet Sarah's brother before he drove with Luke in the car and to make sure Luke arrived back by curfew. But, as far as she knew, Gram would be around. Plus, Kate had been the one who'd encouraged Luke to go out among real people, instead of only interacting with online avatars. Wasn't it better for him to be out with other teens than at home, giving her date with Cole too much thought?

"All right. I'd like a number for her parents, though, so I can confirm with them that this okay. I need a clear itinerary of what movie showing you'll be at, nothing R-rated." The cashier wasn't allowed to sell tickets for R-rated films to minors, but she knew exceptions got made. "You have to be home by ten-thirty. And do I even need to add that I expect you to behave?"

He folded his arms across his chest. "I will if you will."

KATE WOULD HAVE recognized which house was Cole's even if she weren't staring at the street number on the gleaming white mailbox. The sheriff's car in the driveway was a dead giveaway, for starters. But the front yard looked exactly as she would have imagined. The yard was perfectly manicured, hinting at a resident who liked order, but there was nothing fussy or feminine— no flowers or decorative seasonal banners. There were, however, chalk drawings on the sidewalk, a soccer goal set up for practice in the yard, and a glittery purple bike with training wheels leaning up against the house, beneath the shelter of a front porch overhang.

She climbed out of her car, nervously tugging her halter top into place. After her trip to the pool today, she'd toyed with the idea of stopping by Jazz's shop to buy something special to wear. She'd ultimately decided against it, though, having already endured teasing innuendo about her love life from one Tucker sister today. More important, she wanted to feel at ease, comfortable in something she already owned. The green-and-blue halter dress was one of the sexier items she owned, while still being completely appropriate for late June.

The accompanying strapless bra and lacy black panties she wore beneath were slightly less appropriate.

She'd barely knocked when Cole opened the door. He looked incredible in a pair of jeans and an untucked button down shirt. She found his still damp hair and bare feet oddly endearing.

"Right on time," he said, leaning in for a quick kiss as he ushered her inside. "I should have asked earlier, but you're not allergic to seafood are you?"

"Nope. Sounds great—and smells delicious. I brought these for you," she said, stating the obvious as she passed over the pan of walnut fudge brownies she'd baked.

His eyes lit up. "Oh, good. If the pasta doesn't turn out right, we can skip right to this."

She laughed, following him through a living room decorated in warm earth tones to the kitchen. At the sight of the drawings hung on the fridge with magnets and the two pink-edged pony placemats on the table, her heart gave a funny thump. Her thought from earlier in the day haunted her: *What about stepchildren?* She still couldn't imagine ever again exchanging wedding vows. But she had to admit, Cole's daughters tugged her heartstrings. Plus, his being such a good dad was part of his appeal.

"The girls are with your parents?" she asked, leaning against the granite-topped counter.

He nodded. "They're, um, spending the night. Mom thought a sleepover might be fun."

Her cheeks warmed. A sleepover *would* be fun... although there was no way she'd tiptoe into the farmhouse at sunrise, hoping no one had noticed her all-night absence.

"Can I get you a glass of white wine?" he asked.

"Yes, please."

"Just between you and me, I'm usually a beer guy, but white's supposed to go well with shrimp." He grinned as he poured a glass of sauvignon blanc. "I thought I'd shoot for classy tonight. The girls chipped in, too. They haven't cleaned with so much purpose since last December, when they were trying to impress Santa Claus. You should feel honored."

"I definitely do." But there were nerves, too. After all the effort he'd gone to, she hoped she could muster enough appetite to do dinner justice. "Anything I can do to help?" Standing here sipping wine and thinking about how good he looked in jeans felt unbelievably decadent.

He shook his head. "French bread's in the oven, salad's tossed and waiting in the fridge. We should be all ready in a few minutes."

"You thought of everything."

"Including the after-dinner entertainment." With a grin, he pulled open a drawer and pulled out a DVD.

When Kate read the title on the cover, she laughed out loud. "The pilot episode of *Miranda's Rights*?"

"Mom got it for me a couple of birthdays ago, as a joke, and I never even took the cellophane off. If it turns out to be any good, I will feel vindicated. If, on the other hand, it's as terrible as I suspect…" He glanced her way, the heat in his gaze hotter than the blue flames on the stovetop. "Well, then we may have to come up with other ways to entertain ourselves."

NORMALLY, THE SMELL in the diner would have Luke salivating for a double cheeseburger. He wasn't really hungry, though. He'd eaten so much popcorn during the movie that he felt kind of nauseated. Plus, he'd been uncomfortable since they left the theater. Sitting in the backseat of the car with Sarah made his stomach feel funny—even before her cousin Elliot started in on him.

After they'd exited their movie, Elliot had suggested they duck into one of the other theaters for a "bargain double feature."

"The trick is to do it one person at a time, casually," he'd said, "like you're just coming back from the bathroom."

"Nah, we don't have another two hours anyway,"

Sarah's brother had said. "Luke's gotta be home by ten-thirty."

Elliot had rolled his eyes. "What the hell? Doesn't your mom know it's summer? It's not like this is a school night."

Luke hadn't known how to respond. Luckily, Sarah had interrupted to ask if anyone else had recognized an actress in the movie. Conversation shifted to television shows while they waited to be seated at the diner.

When the hostess finally showed them to a table, they passed Rick Jacobs, sharing a platter of buffalo wings with a couple of burly men in baseball caps. Rick nodded hello but didn't intrude. He knew how to give a guy space, unlike Luke's mom. Before she'd allowed him to go out for the night, she'd called Mrs. Pemberton and practically asked for the life history of Sarah's brother. Luke wouldn't have been surprised if she'd had the sheriff run a background check before agreeing that Luke could get in the car with him.

Once they were all seated, Elliot took a renewed interest in Luke. He glanced from Sarah to Luke, an unpleasant grin on his face. "I don't know how I feel about some punk dating my little cousin. How do I know you're good enough for a Pemberton?"

Sarah kicked him under the table. "We're not dating." Her face was bright red as she said it. Was she humiliated by people thinking she and Luke were more than friends?

Elliot ignored her. "She says it was just you and your mom who moved to this Podunk town. What happened to your dad—he take off?"

"Died," Luke snapped. So far, he and Sarah had

none filled the room, and he asked her if she wanted
dance.

She smirked. "Is that your go-to move, Sheriff
rent? Ask a girl to dance, and the next thing you
now, the two of you are making out?"

"Damn, you're on to me. Guess it's time to drop the
retense," he said, taking the CD case from her hand
s he leaned tantalizingly close, "and just skip to the
aking out."

His lips closed over hers, tasting like Cole and choc-
ate, and she went dizzy with bliss. Their kisses were
anguid and unending, the most perfect seduction she
uld imagine. He swept her hair to the side, giving
m better access to kiss her neck and tease her ear-
be with his tongue. She shivered, the lazy pleasure
e'd been enjoying yielding to neediness.

He rolled her back against the pillow, nipping at her
oat as his hand skimmed her ribcage toward her
ast. She ached with the need to be touched there.
the time his palm covered her through her clothes,
couldn't contain a moan. She turned onto her side,
king one leg over his, trying to bring their bod-
closer together, which wasn't easy in a skirt. She
ed her dress was gone. She wished he'd untie the
r top knotted at her nape.

ut then she'd be undressed in front of him, would
love with him.

ell, *yes*, her hormones agreed ecstatically. That
he point. Yet her mind didn't seem to agree. She'd
king love with a man. Who wasn't her husband.
like a macabre sort of virginity; there could only
first time. Eyes burning with conflicting emo-
she rolled back, putting nearly a foot between

avoided having that conversation, and he resented Elliot's asking.

"Oh. That's tough luck, kid." Elliot leaned back,
looking genuinely sorry. Maybe he didn't completely
suck, although Luke wished Elliot didn't view him as
a "kid." There was only a four-year difference between
them. "My dad ran off a couple of years ago. Mom's
not terrible, but you should meet some of the losers she
dates. That's why I visit my aunt and uncle as often
as possible."

Luke was surprised to find himself on common
ground with the guy. "I don't like *my* mom's boyfriend,
either."

"Sheriff Trent?" Sarah turned to him, surprised.
"He seems okay to me."

Elliot disagreed. "That a-hole gave me a speeding
ticket during spring break. I wasn't going that fast.
Any decent dude would've let me off with a warning."

By the time the waitress came to take their orders,
Luke and Elliot had bonded over their shared dislike of
Cole Trent. As Luke talked trash about the guy, he ex-
perienced a brief moment's guilt, picturing Aly's face.
She'd be hurt if she overheard his comments.

But she wasn't here now. It wasn't as though Luke
was saying anything bad about *her*. When the food
came, Luke discovered his appetite had returned. He
plowed through his onion rings, embellishing the story
of how he'd first met the sheriff and his daughters. He
was beginning to think Elliot was a lot like Bobby
Rowe—a good guy to have in your corner, you just
had to impress him first. And Elliot was guffawing at
Luke's shoplifting story.

Luke had another twinge of guilt, recalling that it

was Rick he'd stolen from. *I gave it back. No harm, no foul.*

"So you took stuff right under the sheriff's nose and put it in his own kid's purse?" Elliot cackled. "Priceless. That took guts, Sullivan."

Luke had left out the part about not finding out who Cole was until afterward since the sheriff had been in civilian clothes. "Yeah, but he caught me. Oops, right?" He rolled his eyes, trying to look nonchalant about his brush with the law.

By ten o'clock, Luke was feeling better about the evening. Sarah was quieter than she usually was while barking out locations of loot while they were gaming, but even she had giggled during Luke's story about the gas station heist. He wished he didn't have to go home so soon. Lame curfew. What did his mom care when he got back, anyway? She was probably still out with *him*. Luke's stomach tightened, making him regret the onion rings.

Sarah's brother calculated the bill, and they all dropped cash into the middle of the table. Luke still had a couple of fives left over and tucked them back into his pocket. While they waited for the waitress to bring change, Elliot leaned across the table with a grin. "Hey, Sullivan, know what you should do?"

"What?"

Elliot pointed across the way where an older couple were leaving their booth. As they walked away, the man tossed a bill on the table for a tip. "You should snag that. Bet you could buy a couple of candy bars for that little girl, and the funniest part is, the sheriff would have no idea they were 'stolen.'" He hooted with

laughter, amused by his own scheme. "You show him the receipt!"

Luke frowned. "I don't know." He'd see bar as belonging to the station, not a person ress tonight had done a good job. Swiping was stealing from *her*. What if she needed

Elliot raised an eyebrow. "I thought yo Were you even telling us the truth about before?"

"Lay off," Sarah's brother said. "Let's of here."

"Why, because little Luke has to g beddy-bye time?" Elliot sounded disgust lier solidarity disappearing. "Come on, livan, it's just a few bucks. No one's t breaking into the bank."

Next to Luke, Sarah squared her shou ing all three of them when she said soft

THEY NEVER ACTUALLY got to the soap o a thoroughly delicious dinner of shrin spent so much time discussing music they loaded the plates into the kit wanted to see his CD collection. T cited bands that would be relationshi if they discovered either of them those artists. Cole pulled a couple throw pillows to the floor and th brownies and reminiscing about th each of them had attended.

When Kate ran across a CD never heard of, Cole put in the

them and trying to gulp in air. Damn it. This was no time for a panic attack!

"Kate?" To his credit, Cole didn't crowd her. He paused, searching her gaze. "Was I rushing you? We don't—"

"You didn't do anything wrong. I was enjoying everything we did. I wanted more."

He arched a brow, no doubt wondering why she'd suddenly bolted if she were enjoying his kisses so much. Unfortunately, she didn't know if she could explain without sounding nuts. She wanted to have sex with Cole. She *really* did. And the visceral realization of how much she wanted it had broken her heart.

She sat up, tucking her knees to her chest. "After Damon died, I didn't want to take the sheets off our bed. I knew that we'd slept in them together for the last time, and I didn't want to wash them. It was like… When you lose someone, it seems like it would be all at once. They're alive, then bam, they're not. But that's not how it is. You lose them in a thousand little ways, over and over." A hot tear hit her arm, and she wanted to kick herself. They'd been having a wonderful night, and she was completely ruining it with her maudlin nonsense.

"Kate, it's okay."

She sniffed. "I want…you. But once I sleep with you, it's another way I've said goodbye to him. A really big way." She'd survived painful milestones like her first birthday post-Damon, the first Christmas without him, the smaller moments like the first time she'd picked up the phone and started to call his cell before remembering there'd never again be an answer at the other end. She'd worried about the first time she kissed another man, but kissing Cole had been so effortless and natural. It had given her an unrealistic sense of how easy this would be. "I th-thought I was ready…"

He stood, crossing the room, then returning a moment later with a tissue box.

She took it gratefully but couldn't meet his gaze. What was the point in getting dolled up for a date if she was going to end up red-nosed with mascara pooling down her cheeks?

He knelt in front of her. "Sweetheart, look at me, please."

Right now, the idea of letting him look into her eyes made her feel as exposed as if she were naked. She was trying to psych herself up to accomplish the tiny act of bravery when a jarring sound cut through the jazz still softly playing.

"That's my phone." She shot to her feet, grimly thankful for the interruption. Intellectually, she knew she and Cole would have to discuss this if there were any possibility of them moving forward. But emotionally, she wanted time to put this raging embarrassment behind her before facing him again. The number on her cell phone display was Luke's. Was he calling to let her know he'd made it safely home before curfew?

Maybe it was fortuitous she and Cole had stopped when they did. She couldn't imagine trying to pause in the middle of sex to talk to her son. "H-hello?"

But it wasn't Luke's voice that answered her. "Ms. Sullivan? This is Rick Jacobs, calling on Luke's behalf. I'm at the diner on Main Street, where your son is currently talking to the manager. It might be a good idea for you to come down here."

"Is he okay?"

"Yes, ma'am…but maybe in a little trouble. There seems to be some suspicion that he stole cash off a table, although Luke's insisting the witness misunderstood."

It wasn't my fault this time. How often had she heard statements like that back in Houston? She choked back a sob, recalling her optimism earlier in the day. It seemed her confidence in herself and in her son had been misplaced. "I'm on my way."

Chapter Ten

Luke was beginning to think he was going to hurl the onion rings back up. The flinty-eyed manager who'd hauled him into the stuffy back office clearly didn't believe Luke's story—that a breeze had fluttered the five-dollar bill to the floor and Luke had simply picked it up to put back on the table. Telling the truth would land Sarah in trouble. Luke wasn't about to rat her out.

After saying she would take the tip money, she'd shot him a nervous smile as soon as Elliot was busy looking at his phone. Luke had the impression Sarah was trying to do him a favor so that her cousin would stop harping on him. Luke had wanted to tell her not to, but the words had stuck in his throat. After all, *he'd* been the one bragging about stealing in the first place.

Instead, he'd formulated a plan. He'd let Sarah swipe the money, then replace it with the cash in his pocket once the Pembertons were a few feet ahead of him. No harm, no foul. Except, a nosy customer who'd seen him standing at the table with a five in his hand had misunderstood the situation and accused Luke of stealing. The waitress who'd given him his onion rings with a friendly smile had glared daggers at him and called for the manager, asking that Luke be banned from the diner.

Elliot had glared, too, probably putting together what Luke had really been doing. He'd told the manager he and his cousin had to get Sarah home by curfew. That was when Rick had stepped up, saying that he was a friend of Luke's mother and would call her. The Pembertons had bailed, leaving Luke behind.

Now, Luke sat at the front of the restaurant, where people traditionally waited for a table, with staff members eyeing him like he was a criminal while his mom made the drive from the sheriff's house. Rick sat next to him, not abandoning him like the Pembertons, but not saying much, either. Luke wanted to ask if the man believed him, but it was difficult to get the question out since, technically, Luke wasn't telling the whole truth.

Still, the silence was grating his nerves raw. He sighed as he watched his mom's car turn into the parking lot. As much as he wanted to get out of here, he dreaded facing her. He had an image of himself grounded until he was roughly Gram's age. "Mom is gonna lose her sh—her mind," he amended at Rick's reproachful look.

"Stop giving her reasons to," the man said bluntly.

Luke slouched down, wanting to insist this was all Elliot's fault. The creep had been goading him since before they even got to the diner. *So why didn't you ignore him, genius? Why try to impress him with the stupid candy-bar story?* Not only was his mother going to be mad about Luke stealing, which he hadn't even done, she was going to be ticked that her date had been interrupted. From the goofy smile she'd had all afternoon, he knew she'd really been looking forward to it.

She was not smiling when she walked inside. Her cheeks were blotchy, her eyes overly bright.

"Mom!"

Rick put a hand on his shoulder. "I'm going to have a word with your mother."

The two adults stood off to the side, keeping their voices low. Luke couldn't hear what they were saying, but his stomach sank even lower every time his mom darted a glance his way. He wished he knew whether Rick was putting in a good word for him or throwing him under the bus. He squirmed in his seat, wondering if the man would want his help again for the hospital magic show. Luke had enjoyed that. Performing for those kids had made him feel the same rush of pride he used to get when he showed his comics to classmates who thought the drawings were cool. He missed that.

Finally, Rick squeezed his mom's arm and, with a nod in Luke's direction, left. Next, she had to talk with the manager. Luke gathered from the bits he overheard that, since there wasn't hard evidence that he'd been planning to walk out with the money, the manager didn't feel as though he could ban him for life. However, he stressed that any time Luke came to the diner in the future, he would be watched *very closely*.

How was that fair? Elliot would go back home, in no trouble at all, Sarah got to keep the five dollars she'd taken, but Luke would be treated like a criminal any time he had a craving for onion rings. Which, actually, might never happen again. Those might be ruined for life.

"Let's go." His mother's voice was so soft his ears strained to hear her.

Was it a good sign that she wasn't yelling? Maybe

she just wanted to get him inside the car, away from witnesses. The farm was miles away from Main Street. He imagined his mom shoving him out of the vehicle in some darkened ditch. Even as the picture looped over and over in his mind like a GIF, he knew she'd never do anything like that. *She loves me.*

He swallowed, waiting as she unlocked the car. "How, um, was your date?" He wasn't sure why he asked, but he had to say something. And he didn't want to talk about what had happened in the diner. Besides, if there was even a slim possibility that talking about the sheriff might put that goofy smile back on her face, perhaps she'd be in too good a mood to ground Luke for sixty years.

"Don't you *dare*." Her voice was still low, but it sounded like a growl now, more ominous than it had in the diner. "It's not easy for me, knowing you hate my relationship with Cole, but I respect your right to have feelings on the subject. Have enough respect for me not to stoop to brazen manipulation. It's insulting and dishonest."

"I'm sorry," he mumbled, a little surprised to find that it was true.

They'd been driving for five minutes before he spoke again. The tremor in his voice made him feel like a crybaby, but he couldn't help it. "I didn't take that money, I promise."

Her silence was louder than any of the video games she told him to turn down because she could hear them even through his headset. "Give me one reason why I should believe you."

Because it's the truth. But it was only part of the truth. He'd screwed up. Staring out the window into the darkness, he promised himself that he'd find a way to make it up to her.

KATE HAD BEEN so caught up in the emotional upheaval of her evening that she'd completely forgotten to call Gram. When her cell phone rang and Gram's picture flashed on the screen, shame filled her. It was now fifteen minutes past when Luke was supposed to have been home. Gram was probably worried sick.

"Luke's with me," she said as soon as she answered the phone. "There was…a bit of a problem at the diner where he and his friends stopped, so I'm giving him a ride home."

"Oh, well, I'm glad to hear that! Not the problem part, of course. But that you know where he is and I don't have to break the news to you that he missed curfew."

"We'll be home in ten minutes," Kate said, "maybe less."

"If it's all the same to you, dear, I'm going to turn in. See you in the morning? Oh, and in case I forget, Mrs. Abernathy apparently referred you to some other moms she knows. You had two calls from parents who want to meet with you. I wrote their numbers on the pad by the phone."

"Thanks, Gram." Kate bit her lip, thinking about the latest trouble Luke was in and the trouble they'd collectively caused since arriving. "Before I meet with any other prospective clients, are you *sure* you're okay with this parade of people in and out of the house?" Tomorrow was shaping up to be a busy day.

Gram chuckled. "Are you kidding? I haven't had so many visitors in years! Patch is in heaven." She sighed. "It's been lonely since I lost Jim. You and Luke have done so much to change that. I'll miss you if the two of you ever move."

"We're not planning on going anywhere," Kate said.

"Well…you never know, dear. You're still young. You may build a home elsewhere."

A home, or a family? From the sly, expectant tone in Gram's tone, she was hoping tonight's date with Cole had gone well. Thinking about it still mortified Kate. She'd wanted him so badly, yet…when she could have had him, she'd freaked out. Sophisticated sex goddess, she was not.

Kate wished her grandmother a good night, then disconnected. Ever since Rick Jacobs had called her, she'd been too furious with Luke's bad judgment to question why he'd bothered to steal a few bucks anyway. After all, this was the same kid who'd once inexplicably snatched a candy bar. But now, she couldn't help wondering, had his getting in trouble tonight been an attempt to sabotage her date?

She tried not to think that, on some level, she might have been glad for the excuse to leave.

Friday passed without Kate talking to Cole. As he'd warned when he said Thursday was their best option for dinner, his Friday was pretty busy. As was hers. So she managed to escape the day without any cringeworthy rehashing of what had happened between them.

He left her two voice mails, and she sent him a text assuring that she and Luke were both okay and that she and Cole would talk soon. He'd wanted to come with her last night to the diner, but she'd refused. Partly because she'd desperately needed space and also because it was awkward when your boyfriend was the sheriff and your son was exhibiting criminal tendencies.

Now that Friday was over, Kate wanted to slip into

the oblivion of slumber and forget everything for a few hours. Heaven knew she should be exhausted. Last night, she hadn't been able to sleep a wink. But two hours after she'd retired to bed, sleep still eluded her. *Insomnia: 2, Sullivan: 0.*

Aggravated, she flipped over on her stomach. She never slept on her stomach, but she'd already tried both sides and lying on her back. Nothing was working. She had too many thoughts and worries buzzing through her, as well as a growing regret that she'd avoided speaking to Cole. *Coward.*

He'd been so patient and understanding with her, but patience wasn't infinite. How long would his last before he decided to wash his hands of her and find someone with fewer issues?

In addition to her emotional turmoil over the sheriff, she still had to decide what to do with her son. At lunch today, he'd broken down and told a convoluted story about how Sarah's cousin had bullied Sarah into stealing the five dollars. Either Luke was lying or Sarah was a thief or her cousin was a bully—possibly a combination of all three. While the details were fuzzy, she had the sense that he'd acted out of misguided teen nobility to protect Sarah, probably to make amends for the cruel way he'd spoken to her earlier in the week. But, honestly, when was her kid going to start learning from his mistakes and show better judgment? Had she moved him away from one peer group full of bad influences just to get him involved with another that was equally questionable?

Okay, lying on her stomach wasn't doing a damned thing to soothe her. She was half-heartedly entertaining the notion of a shot of whiskey when the phone rang, causing her to sit straight up in bed. It was pretty late for a call, especially in Cupid's Bow. Across the hall, she heard gentle snoring in her grandmother's room, so she hurried to the kitchen to grab the phone before the caller woke the entire household.

"Hello?" she said, keeping her voice low.

"Kate?" The woman on the other end of the phone sounded unsteady. "It's Gayle Trent. I—"

"Oh, God." She clutched the receiver so tightly the plastic creaked in protest. Her heart stopped. "What happened to him?" There was only one reason the sheriff's mother would call her in the dead of the night.

"He's all right, dear. He's in stable condition, and the doctor says he may not even have to stay the night. But I thought you should know."

Kate was suddenly shaking so badly she couldn't stand. She sat straight down on the floor, not bothering with the distance between her and the nearest chair. "Cole's at the hospital?"

"Yes. Deputy Thomas told us they answered a domestic disturbance call tonight. Cole was stabbed. An...an anterior stab wound, the doctor said. He lost a lot of blood, but he's going to be..." Her voice caught, broke.

There was a sob and rustling, then a male voice. "Kate? It's Will. I'm here with Mom and Dad. Cole's going to be all right," he said fiercely. "They're just running tests to make sure there was no perforation or occult trauma. We should be able to see him soon."

"I'll be there in ten minutes," Kate said.

He laughed, a brief rusty sound. "You can't make it to the hospital from Whippoorwill Creek in ten minutes."

The hell she couldn't.

But reality caught up to her as she fished her car keys out of her purse. For starters, she probably shouldn't show up to the hospital in nothing but a nightgown. And it would be irresponsible to leave in the middle of the night without writing a note that said where she'd gone and when she expected to be back. Plus, the last thing she wanted was to cause any accidents in her haste to get to the hospital, so she resolved to stick to the speed limit. More or less.

It was a fight, though, to keep her foot from mashing the accelerator through the floor. Her rush was twofold. Not only did she need to get to the hospital, to see Cole with her own two eyes, she needed to outrun the horrible, ice-cold déjà vu running through her veins. *I can't do this again. I can't.*

She clung to Will's assurance that Cole would be okay. This was completely different than when she'd rushed to the hospital the night Damon was shot—too late to say goodbye. The memories haunted her, overlapping with reality, and by the time she parked in the visitor's deck, scalding tears poured down her face.

Will was waiting for her, his handsome face haggard with worry. But he tried to cover his own concern with a smile. "No tears, darlin'. My brother is ornery, much harder to take down than this. I promise. Mom and Dad are in with him now. He asked me to take you straight back when you arrived."

She mumbled something that might have been thank you, but she wasn't sure. Words had lost meaning. She was only processing half of what Will said. She felt as if she were trying to walk on the ocean floor. Sound and movement were distorted, and she felt cold all over.

The world didn't start to right itself again until she stepped into the partitioned room where Cole sat on a hospital bed with an IV in his arm. His family stepped out to give them a moment of privacy, and Kate went straight to him, running her hand over his bare chest, needing to feel the solid heat of him. Normally, she appreciated any chance to see him shirtless, but the large white bandage covering the side of his torso made her want to vomit. She tried to muffle her cry with her hand and failed miserably.

"Kate, I'm okay." He started to put an arm around her, then cast an impatient glance at the machines monitoring his vitals. He wasn't especially mobile, and he had to be in pain. "Look at me, I'm okay."

"This time!" What about the next time someone was drunk and disorderly? Or if he pulled over the wrong motorist? Or the day some crackpot figured out how to successfully get a gun into the courthouse? "You were lucky."

His lips quirked in a wry half smile. "If getting stabbed is your idea of good luck, I'd hate to—"

"Please don't joke. Not about this. Not about your safety." She was backing away from him as she spoke, as if her being here was somehow dangerous to him. *No, his being close is a danger to you.* What had she been thinking? How could she let herself fall for another man, especially the sheriff? She'd known it was a bad idea, but he'd won her over with his patient coaxing and his devilish blue eyes and how great he was with his girls.

"I can only imagine how hard this is for you," he said, holding out a hand, trying to draw her back to him. "I wish my mom hadn't called you, but—"

"Her not calling wouldn't have changed the fact that you're hurt. Just like my ignoring the risks won't save me from getting hurt. I knew better!" She glanced at him and for a second, in the double vision of her tears, there were two Coles.

Both were shaking their heads at her. "Don't do this," he insisted. "You're overreacting because of your past, because you lost Damon."

"I'm not reacting to my past—it's too late to change that—but I am trying to safeguard my future. Because I finally, vividly, understand how much you could break my heart. I can't…" *I can't do this again.* She swallowed hard, determined to choke out the last words. He at least deserved to hear her say them. "Goodbye, Cole."

WHEN LUKE GOT up Saturday morning, he knew as soon as he left his room that something was wrong. On the way to the bathroom, he heard mom and Gram talking in weirdly hushed voices, the kind he recognized from after his dad's death. His first fear was that they were talking about *him*. What if that stupid five dollars in tip money turned out to be his mom's breaking point and she was considering something drastic, like sending him off to military school or something? Then he heard the words *stab* and *hospital*.

"Gayle called me with an update while you were in the shower," Gram said.

Gayle Trent? Luke suddenly realized that they were discussing the sheriff. Cole Trent had been stabbed? Panic twisted in Luke's gut. Aly and Mandy shouldn't grow up without a dad. No kid should have to grow up without a dad!

When his grandmother added, "He's at home and doing better," Luke sagged in relief, reaching out to support himself against the wall.

"But he's plenty ticked off," Gram added. "I can't believe you dumped a stab victim while he was still in the hospital." She sounded disappointed. There was a lot of that going around in the house lately.

Wait, Mom had broken up with the sheriff? Luke wasn't sure how to feel about that. He hadn't liked Cole—it was impossible to like someone you suspected was trying to get your mother in bed. But she'd looked so happy the other day.

"Gram, I can't. Not again. I made myself way too vulnerable. I suppose I should be glad Luke hated us dating. What if he'd gotten attached? He's already lost so much. How would it have affected him if he and Cole bonded, then we broke up? Or Cole got… If he…"

She was crying. Luke fisted his hands in helpless frustration.

Gram's voice was soothing now, not chiding. "I understand the desire to protect yourself and your son. But how much can you realistically shelter yourself? Just getting into a car can be dangerous, yet people do it every day."

"People need to get places. I don't *need* to date the town sheriff."

It got very quiet in the kitchen, and Luke wondered if they were done discussing the subject. He should go. He was in enough trouble without his mother catching him eavesdropping. Just as he turned to leave, he heard Gram make one last point.

"I love you, dear, and it was a tragedy your husband was taken from you so young, but you're not the only one who's lost the man you love. Don't you think I'd give anything I had for one more day with my Jim? Even if I knew I'd lose him again afterward, I'd cherish that limited time. Because, really, that's all any of us have, even in the best of situations—limited time."

It was a morbid thought for a sunny Saturday morning, but, as Luke crept away, he couldn't get the words out of his head.

ALTHOUGH THE DOCTOR had only technically cleared Cole for desk duty, to reduce the risk of his popping his stitches, by Thursday Cole was desperate for more to do. An abyss of misery yawned at his feet, waiting to swallow him whole whenever he was inactive. Thankfully, his brother took pity on him.

"You can't help set up the booth," Will stressed when he picked up Cole in his truck. "But you can supervise and delegate. The guys will listen to you. Then once we're in good shape for the festival kickoff tomorrow, I'll buy you lunch."

This week was all about festival preparation, but Cole had never cared less about the damned Watermelon Festival. This year, it was simply a reminder that his date for Sunday never wanted to see him again. And to add insult to injury, in about forty-eight hours, he would probably be purchased for a date with Becca Johnston.

Hell, maybe he should just go out with her anyway. He'd say this for her, she was stalwart. Not the type to head for the hills over something as minor as a paltry stabbing.

As soon as he'd seen Kate's pale face in the hospital, he'd known. They were over, practically before they'd begun. He wasn't sure which of them he was angrier at—her, for prioritizing fear over what they could have had together; or himself, because she'd warned him since day one that she was still too fragile for a relationship with him and he hadn't listened.

Trying to push Kate from his mind, he climbed out of Will's truck, calling greetings to other firemen who were helping erect a booth for safety demonstrations and the stage for the auction that would ultimately benefit the fire department. For about half an hour, he actually managed to convince himself he was being useful. It was the closest he'd come to approaching cheerful in days.

But it was damned difficult to push someone from your mind when she was walking toward you with a hesitant expression and a banner painted with pink letters that were outlined in green and flecked with black. Seeing her knocked him so off guard that it took him a second to realize the letters were supposed to represent slices of watermelon.

"Hi." She approached carefully, as if he were a feral animal. Truthfully, there had been moments over the past few days when that seemed like an accurate description of his mood.

"Hi." He let his gaze flick in her direction without lingering on her. Looking at her was too painful. "So, you got pressed into volunteer service, huh?"

"Gram thought I could use the…"

Distraction. Did that mean she'd been moping around the farm? Was it possible Kate was missing him as much as he missed her?

"How's the wound healing?" she asked. "Gram's

been giving me updates from your mom, but I guess I need to hear it for myself. How are you?"

He made himself meet her gaze then, letting her see exactly how he was doing. He was miserable. She might be worried about the stabbing, but her words to him at the hospital had sliced through him with far more pain and destruction than that blade.

"I…" She dropped her gaze, but not before he caught the tears glistening on her lashes. "I'm sorry I interrupted. I saw you here and had to check to see if you were okay."

No. I'm not. "I'll live." Which was more than she allowed herself to do. Cole knew seeing him in the hospital had to have been emotionally wrenching, but in retrospect, he couldn't help wondering if she would have found a reason to end things anyway. She'd obviously been conflicted at his house Thursday night, then she'd avoided him the following day. If his injury hadn't prompted her mad dash to the hospital, would she have continued to avoid him? Would she have gone longer and longer without returning his calls and eventually found an excuse, such as her son's antics, to keep from being Cole's date to the festival?

Although the idea of her with another man caused Cole to grind his teeth in jealous fury, he would rather see her on another guy's arm than watch her hide behind fear and the hostilities of a thirteen-year-old. Kate was a passionate, bighearted woman with a lot of love to give. If only she were brave enough to let herself.

The silence between them had passed awkward about six seconds ago, and Cole sighed, knowing he should cut her loose. "Thanks for checking on me. I hope you and Luke have fun at the festival this weekend. Don't let your grandmother or anyone else work you too hard."

"Thanks. I... I hope you feel better soon."

And then she was gone. He wanted so badly to chase after her, to implore her to change her mind. But he'd been coaxing and cajoling since they'd met. There was a line between patiently wooing, and stalking. Besides, he had his pride—or at least the tattered remains of it.

Cupid's Bow was a small town. She knew where to find him if she changed her mind.

LUKE WAS SURROUNDED by what felt like hundreds of happy people—and he hadn't even thought Cupid's Bow *had* hundreds of people. Maybe some of the people playing midway games, signing up for the watermelon-eating contest and buying giant turkey legs dripping in grease were out-of-towners. He didn't care so much about their origins as he did their collective good mood. He was desperately hoping it would rub off on his mother.

She was starting to scare him. He knew she was crying when no one was around to see; her puffy, red eyes were unmistakable. But she seemed determined to have fun at the festival with him. She'd been smiling all day, but not a real smile. It was like he'd gone to town with a creepy animatronic version of his mother.

Even now, she was staring at him with that fixed smile and blank eyes. "What do you want to do now? There are some arts-and-crafts demonstrations. I know you might be a little old for some of those, but you've always had so much natural talent. Or we could try out some of the rides, although I'm not sure my dinner's had enough time to settle," she warned.

"Or we could just go home," he said. She seemed pretty sad there, but, somehow, out among all these happy-happy festivalgoers, it was even worse.

"This early?" she asked. "Are you sure?"

He shrugged. "You said it was a four-day thing. We should pace ourselves."

"All right." Was it his imagination, or was there a hint of relief behind her plastic expression?

They crossed between a snack shack and a small stage where regional choirs were performing patriotic songs, headed in the direction of the parking lot down the street. It wasn't until they'd left some of the noise behind him that Luke realized someone was calling his name. He and his mom turned at the same time, and he felt a wave of surprise when he saw Sarah running down the sidewalk after him. They hadn't really spoken since the night at the diner. Seeing her now, he felt a flash of joy—he'd missed her—tempered by wariness. He didn't even know if he was allowed to talk to her, or if she'd joined Bobby Rowe on his mom's forbidden list.

"Hey," he said noncommittally, darting a nervous look in his mom's direction.

It took him a second to realize there was an adult trailing Sarah at a much more sedate speed.

"That's my mom," Sarah explained. "We tried to catch up with you earlier in the crowd, but lost you during the parade. Luke, I owe you an apology, and your mother one, too, for the trouble I caused. I've already told my parents about what happened. Mrs. Sullivan, Luke didn't take that money." She hung her head. "I did. It was stupid. My cousin Elliot more or less dared one of us to, and I should have just told him to shut up. Luke was only trying to put the money back."

Next to him, his mother shifted and he was relieved to see the freaky masklike expression disappear. She looked like herself again. "You were telling me the truth. I'm sorry I didn't believe you more wholeheartedly."

"I'm sorry you've had so many reasons to doubt me," he mumbled.

Mrs. Pemberton was introducing herself to his mom and apologizing for Elliot's role in everything. "My nephew hasn't always been a troublemaker, but he's not taking his parents' divorce well. Rest assured, my children won't be going anywhere unsupervised with him for a long while. In fact, they're both currently grounded, although I have to make an exception for the Watermelon Festival."

Luke's mom managed a small laugh. "Absolutely. After all, it's in the town bylaws."

"Well, we won't keep you," Mrs. Pemberton said. "Sarah told me last night what really happened, and when we spotted you today…"

"I wanted to fix things," Sarah said shyly. "I hope we can be friends again."

Luke grinned. "You forgave me for being a jerk on the phone. I guess I can forgive you for being a notorious criminal. But…we should probably avoid the diner next time we go out for burgers."

"I'll text you when I'm not grounded anymore."

"She's a nice girl," his mom said as they resumed their walk to the car. "I'm glad to see you making friends in Cupid's Bow."

His mother had friends, too. She liked hanging out

with Crystal and Jazz. But he wasn't stupid. He knew the person who meant the most to her in this town was the sheriff.

All week, Luke had been cringing at his mom's secret crying jags, which reminded him of when his dad died. But in a way, these were worse. No power on earth could have brought his dad back. There was nothing they could do.

But her relationship with Sheriff Trent? In theory, that was fixable. So maybe he should follow Sarah's example and do something to fix it.

Chapter Eleven

On Saturday, Kate woke to a truly horrendous stench wafting into her room. It smelled as if someone was throwing old tires onto a bonfire nearby. Just as she was swinging her feet to the floor in order to go investigate, there was a knock on her bedroom door.

Before she had a chance to answer, Luke peeked his head inside. "I brought you breakfast in bed," he informed her.

Oh, good Lord. He was the bearer of the stench. He came into her room with a tray that included a glob of purple she assumed was grape jelly with bread somewhere underneath it and charred eggs.

She swallowed hard. "Wow. To what do I owe this… surprise?"

"Mom, we need to talk about your love life."

"Uh…" It generally took her brain about an hour to start functioning properly. She was ill-equipped to take on a subject fraught with that many landmines.

"Look, I know this is a heinous topic for both of us," he said as he shoved the tray into her hands, "but sometimes people have to discuss things even when it's not comfortable."

She blinked, relatively certain he was parroting

back something she'd recently said to him. *He listens!* Who knew?

"About Sheriff Trent—"

"You don't have to worry about that relationship anymore," she assured him. "That's over."

"But you love him. Don't you?"

There it was, the question she'd been trying not to ask herself. Fired at her from her thirteen-year-old with the precision of a sniper. "I…" Was it too late to pull the blankets over her head and pretend she was asleep?

"I think you should go for it, Mom."

"*You do?* Who are you and what have you done with my son?"

Shamefaced, Luke sat on the mattress next to her. "I guess I've been kind of obnoxious about the whole thing. When I miss Dad, I like to think about the three of us together. It's comforting to remember you with him. Seeing you with someone else…well, it made me want to blow chunks."

"So why the change in her heart?" she asked. This week, she'd fielded well-meaning lectures from Gram, Crystal and even Brody Davenport when she'd run into him at the supermarket, although his had been far more subtle. But the very last person she'd expected to encourage a reconciliation with Cole was her son.

"As much as I hate seeing you with the sheriff," Cole said, "it turns out, seeing you *without* him is even worse."

She bit the inside of her cheek, feeling guilty. She'd made an attempt to act normal this week, not inflicting her misery on the rest of the household, but she'd obviously failed.

He fidgeted, not meeting her gaze. "Do you remember when you told me we were moving to Cupid's Bow and I complained all the time?"

"*All* the time," she agreed. "Twenty-four-seven."

"Every time I whined about coming here, you told me to think positive. So why aren't you, Mom? It seems like you're making decisions based on worst-case scenarios."

My God, he's right. Was that really the example she wanted to set for him? Gram had pointed out rather pragmatically that everyone had limited time, and no one could foresee when that time might come to an end. So did Kate want to spend whatever years she had joyously embracing life—and love—and teaching her son to do the same? Or did she want to cower in fear, shying away from risks?

A smile spread across her face, and she felt lighter than she had in days. "You know, kiddo, for a thirteen-year-old, you can be pretty wise."

He grinned, looking pleased with himself. "Does this mean you'll get him back?"

She prayed it wasn't too late after she'd rejected Cole when he was wounded. "First, we need a real breakfast. Then we need a plan."

WHEN THE AUCTIONEER called his name, Cole limped out onstage. He'd been on his feet for what felt like forty-eight hours straight and had spent so much time shifting his weight to compensate for the pain in his side that he'd made his leg sore. Plus, there was always the slim hope that if he looked like damaged goods, women wouldn't bid on him. Let them save their money for guys like Jarrett and Will.

Or not, he thought with an inward sigh as Becca Johnston belted out a bid. Cole scanned the assembled crowd, hoping this would end quickly so he could go grab a hamburger. His gaze snagged on one familiar face.

Kate was here? He'd hoped she would stay away. Their last encounter had been awkward enough. But he supposed she was just doing her civic duty.

He was so stunned to hear her declare, "Forty dollars!" in a voice that rang like a bell, he almost toppled over. Forty? The highest winning bid so far had been eighty-seven bucks. Cole was almost halfway there. Why would she bid on him? She had to know he wouldn't hold her to their previous agreement, not now that she'd walked away from the possibility of a future with him.

Another woman called out forty-five dollars, and Becca immediately countered with sixty. The auctioneer looked at Cole with blatant approval, then attempted to whip the women into a bidding frenzy. By the time they passed the hundred dollar mark, Cole's heart was in his throat. His gaze was locked on Kate's as he tried to decipher her motives, but he couldn't tell anything from here. Except that her smile was the most beautiful sight in all of Cupid's Bow.

When Becca Johnston reached one hundred and twenty-five dollars, Cole wanted to slump in despair. Kate hadn't wanted him when she could have him for free; surely she wouldn't pay triple digits for the privilege.

"One forty."

"One sixty!"

"One sixty-five." Kate's eyes never left his.

"One hundred and ninety dollars," Becca said, studying her manicure as if she could do this all day.

An expectant hush fell across the crowd. "Two hundred," Kate said. But her voice trembled slightly. Piano teachers didn't make tons of money. On either side of her, Jazz and Crystal were digging through their pockets and purses.

"Two hundred and fifteen." Becca sounded aggrieved now. Her hands were on her hips, and she was glaring in Kate's direction.

Kate squared her shoulders and lifted her chin. "All I have to offer is two hundred and twenty-eight dollars…and faith. Faith in love and second chances and the courage to pursue happiness. I'm just sorry I hadn't saved up enough of it before now."

Cole's heart was bursting with pride in her—and joy over her words. If he weren't worried about popping his stitches, he would have jumped down from the stage already to kiss her. A loud sniffle distracted him, and he glanced in surprise at Becca Johnston.

"Oh, just give it to her," Becca said, wiping at her eyes with the side of her hand. "I can't top that."

As the audience broke into applause, Kate ran to the edge of the stage. Will was suddenly there to give her a boost up onto the platform.

Then she was in Cole's arms, and his leg didn't hurt anymore. Neither did his side. Or his heart.

He pulled her close for a kiss, murmuring, "I love you," against her lips.

"I love you, too. I thought it was too soon to say, but what am I waiting for? Life is precious. And I want to spend as much of it with you as I can."

"Even when it gets scary?" he asked.

The specter of fear crossed her face, but she smiled anyway. "When it gets scary, you'll just have to hold me and make it all better."

"Deal."

AS LUKE JOINED the rest of them at the shaded picnic table, he saw the sheriff steal another kiss from his mom. Somehow, it didn't seem as gross as it had before. Maybe because Luke was in such a good mood.

"I never thought I'd win a trophy for anything besides video games," he said, setting the gold cup on top of the table.

His mom laughed. "I don't know what they were thinking, letting a teenage boy participate in an eating contest. The rest of the competition didn't stand a chance."

Gram grinned. "Lots of winners this weekend. Luke won the watermelon-eating trophy, you won a date with the sheriff..."

"Ha," Kate scoffed. "I didn't win it. I paid for it."

Cole put his arm around her. "I promise to be worth every penny."

Okay, now they were getting too sappy. To distract himself, Luke turned to Aly on his other side. She was coloring on a sheet of paper. "Whatcha drawing?" he asked.

"Us." She pushed the paper toward him so that he could see the representation of him, the twins, Cole and his mom, all holding hands and smiling underneath a rainbow.

"Hey, you only used the sparkly crayons on the

adults," he commented, noticing how the tallest of the two stick figures shimmered. "What about the rest of us?"

She shrugged, then pointed to where his mom was whispering something to the sheriff. "Don't they seem extra-sparkly?"

"Yeah. Yeah, they do." He grinned from ear to ear. If anyone had told him a month ago that his mom would look this happy—or that Luke would be having fun in Cupid's Bow—Luke would have assumed it was some weird practical joke.

"Daddy, can I go with Nana to get an ice cream?" Mandy asked suddenly, spotting her grandparents at the nearby frozen desserts vendor.

"Sure," Cole answered, barely taking his eyes off Luke's mom.

Aly frowned. "But she had a funnel cake a little while ago. And a popsicle! We're never allowed to have that much junk food."

Luke laughed, lowering his voice to a conspiratorial whisper. "Want to know a secret about adults? Sometimes when they're in a *really* good mood, they give permission for stuff they would normally say no to."

"Really?" Her face brightened, and she scampered off the bench, inserting herself between her dad and "Miss Kate" to show them her drawing. Once she had their full attention, she beamed up at them. "So, about my pony…"

* * * * *

Be sure to look for more stories in Tanya Michaels's
CUPID'S BOW, TEXAS *series*
coming in 2016,
wherever Harlequin books are sold!